"You'll consider it?"

Mike's jaw tightened as if biting down on further arguments.

Paige made some quick calculations. His proposal made a lot of sense. With her baby due in early February, she couldn't expect a roommate to stay past the first of the year, anyway. If he moved out in September, she could decorate the nursery at her leisure, and she wouldn't inconvenience some innocent roommate who expected to stay indefinitely.

That left one problem. A big one. Around him, her pregnancy-heightened senses quivered at the infusion of masculinity into the atmosphere. They'd be sharing a bathroom, lounging in the living room in bathrobes…and the mere prospect of seeing Mike in a swimsuit made her breasts tighten.

How could she put this delicately? "You and I don't exactly have a platonic relationship," P~~ murmured. "Living together i~~

Dear Reader,

Welcome to Safe Harbor, California, where doctors at the medical center help women have the babies they long for. Sometimes, those doctors are having the babies themselves!

When private detective Mike Aaron and obstetrician Paige Brennan first met in *Falling for the Nanny*, he offended her by describing her as an Amazon. Naturally, a romance writer can see that these two strong-minded individuals were destined to fall in love.

But as always, I like to put a twist on things to make them fun for the reader, and for me as a writer. In *The Detective's Accidental Baby*, which featured Mike's brother Sherlock, we learned that Mike doesn't want kids but has become a sperm donor. Paige, however, wants a baby very much.

In *The Baby Dilemma*, their worlds collide. She's about to get pregnant with his child in a high-tech way. The fact that they also become lovers adds a delicious complication. Will love bridge the gap? I hope you'll enjoy finding out!

Best,

Jacqueline Diamond

The Baby Dilemma

JACQUELINE DIAMOND

TORONTO NEW YORK LONDON
AMSTERDAM PARIS SYDNEY HAMBURG
STOCKHOLM ATHENS TOKYO MILAN MADRID
PRAGUE WARSAW BUDAPEST AUCKLAND

Recycling programs
for this product may
not exist in your area.

ISBN-13: 978-0-373-75404-5

THE BABY DILEMMA

Copyright © 2012 by Jackie Hyman

This edition published by arrangement with Harlequin Books S.A.

For questions and comments about the quality of this book
please contact us at Customer_eCare@Harlequin.ca

® and TM are trademarks of the publisher. Trademarks indicated with
® are registered in the United States Patent and Trademark Office, the
Canadian Trade Marks Office and in other countries.

www.Harlequin.com

Printed in U.S.A.

ABOUT THE AUTHOR

After overcoming fertility problems to have two wonderful sons, Jacqueline Diamond has maintained a lifelong interest in doctors, babies and the miracle of birth. As for love, she's shared that for more than 30 years with her husband, Kurt. A former reporter and editor at two newspapers and the Associated Press, Jackie has written some 90 romances and mysteries, as well as *How to Write a Novel in One (Not-so-easy) Lesson.* Jackie, who received a Career Achievement Award from *RT Book Reviews*, lives in Orange County, California, and posts free writing tips plus information about her books at www.jacquelinediamond.com. You can email her at jdiamondfriends@yahoo.com.

Books by Jacqueline Diamond
HARLEQUIN AMERICAN ROMANCE

For my writing students

Chapter One

"I'm beginning to think there should be a special place in the wedding ceremony for the bride's obstetrician," Dr. Paige Brennan said as she washed up following surgery.

"I'm glad you'll be there Saturday, even though I'm no-where near my due date." Erica Benford, the nurse who had assisted during the operation, beamed at her. Ever since announcing her engagement, she'd been glowing brightly enough to illuminate the entire Safe Harbor Medical Center complex.

The June bride was a mere four months along. Paige hoped her pregnancy turned out as well as that of Dr. Nora Franco, who had marched down the aisle exactly a year earlier at the same stage of pregnancy, also with Paige in attendance. Five months later, Paige had delivered Nora's darling little boy.

Weddings might be beautiful, but in Paige's opin-ion, babies were in a class by themselves. She hoped her friends didn't guess how fiercely she wished she were the one carrying a child-to-be.

As for the man waiting at the altar, Paige considered him optional. With the modern technology available through Safe Harbor's fertility program, a woman could choose the father of her baby anonymously, confident that he'd been screened for his medical and psychological health. She had a choice of his physical characteristics, interests and accomplishments, too.

With any luck... She stopped her hand from drifting to her abdomen.

This was the hopeful part of the month. Her first insemination hadn't produced results, but you couldn't expect to get pregnant in one try. And her period was two days late. *Maybe this time...*

"I can't wait to see Lock in a tuxedo," Erica chattered on. Her fiancé, a private detective appropriately named Sherlock, was devoted to her and to their developing baby, eagerly attending every appointment and peppering Paige with questions.

"I'm sure he'll look smashing, but everyone's eyes will be on the bride," Paige reminded her. "You are taking a few days off to get ready, aren't you?"

"How can I? We've got a packed surgical schedule."

"It's only Tuesday. I'm sure the hospital could arrange a substitute on Thursday and Friday."

"And let everyone down? As it is, I'll be gone for a week." Erica was nothing if not dedicated. "I feel guilty staying away that long."

"Take my advice. Enjoy your honeymoon and don't give a second thought to work," Paige advised. "Speaking as your doctor, I don't want you to push yourself too hard. Turn off your cell phone, ignore your email and tell Lock to do the same."

"He might have cases pending," Erica countered.

"Let his brother handle it." Paige waved a hand dismissively, scattering droplets of water. "Oh, sorry."

"Lock and Mike are partners in the agency," Erica noted. "They both have obligations. And our financial future is partly tied up in its success."

"It's your honeymoon. Don't let anyone or anything

intrude. Where are you going, anyway?" Quickly Paige added, "Or it might be a good idea to keep that a secret."

"The Grand Canyon," Erica said blithely. "Then we're going to spend a few days in Las Vegas."

"Sounds like fun. Just be sure to rest when you feel tired."

"Yes, Doctor!" The nurse grinned.

"Glad you agree." Paige dried off and went out, buoyed by Erica's high spirits.

In the hallway, she passed a suite set aside for the fertility project. The hospital in this small Southern California beach community had been revamped a few years ago to specialize in treating women and babies, and the fertility program was its centerpiece. When plans to acquire a separate building for those services fell through, the specialized labs and other facilities had been installed throughout the existing hospital, including the sperm collection rooms here on the second floor.

This place had special meaning for Paige. A meaning that was very private and filled with promise.

She rounded a corner and halted abruptly, her good mood fading. What was *he* doing here?

As detective Mike Aaron fiddled with something on the staff bulletin board located by the nurses' station, he didn't appear to notice Paige. Although tempted to change course and slip off without speaking, she refused to be intimidated, even by a six-foot-four guy who was presumably packing a gun beneath his sports jacket. At six feet herself, Paige could hold her own.

Mike glanced over. Surprise flickered in his steely eyes. "Ah. We meet again."

"That bulletin board is for staff. You shouldn't be reading it." To her embarrassment, Paige realized he might be posting some announcement about the bridal couple, at whose wedding he would serve as best man. "Unless this relates to staff."

"Just passing by." In that cocky grin, she saw a hint of smart-aleck adolescence, although he had to be in his mid-thirties. He ought to adopt a grown-up attitude to match that hard, muscular body of his.

Not that she knew him very well, aside from the fact that he was Lock Vaughn's foster brother, but in a small town like Safe Harbor, it was hard to avoid running into people. The first time they'd met, a year ago at Nora's wedding, he'd rudely referred to Paige as an Amazon. Then at the beach, he'd ambled away from a party to comment on how a redhead like her needed to wear more sunscreen. Last month at the supermarket, he'd appeared out of nowhere, scanned her cart and informed her that a doctor ought to have the sense to buy more vegetables and less pasta.

Her bossy oldest sister, Juno, would have ordered Paige to give thanks for having a man interested in her. Their middle sister, Maeve, would probably claim the universe was throwing him in Paige's path. Thank goodness they were both in Texas and, for the past six months, had left Paige alone. Which was exactly what she wished Mike Aaron would do.

"I don't know what's running through your mind but it looks interesting," he said.

"Nothing that concerns you." Not exactly a lie. Her thoughts were none of his business, even if he did figure into them.

"Are you sure about that?" Mike made no attempt to hide the way his gaze swept her tan blouse beneath the white coat, down the length of her slacks to the brown sling-backs decorated with a row of tiny shells. "Unusual shoes. Quite a beach girl, aren't you?"

"Just because I ran into you there once…"

"Wearing a memorable bikini," Mike murmured.

And *he'd* been wearing a memorable pair of tight trunks. *No place to hide a gun under those,* she thought, and felt her cheeks burn at the thought.

"Redheads shouldn't blush," Mike remarked. "It shows all over." He was focusing on the thin line of chest visible beneath her V-neck.

"I suppose blonds like you never blush." The moment the words were out, she heard how lame they sounded.

"I consider my hair light brown."

"Whatever." It was sandy, in her opinion, but she refrained from any further comments about his appearance. The man already thought the world revolved around him.

Then she spotted the slip of paper in his hand. It had obviously been torn from the ad for a housemate that she'd posted on the board, and it held her phone number.

Following the direction of her gaze, Mike hoisted the slip like a trophy. "What a pleasant discovery that you live half a block from the beach. I love the sea breeze and the sound of the ocean."

"So?" She folded her arms.

"For some inexplicable reason, my current roommate is kicking me out of the house. Something about him and his bride wanting privacy."

Oh, rats. "I'm looking for a female roommate," Paige improvised.

"It doesn't say that."

"It's implied." Actually, it hadn't been, until now.

"What happened to your old roommate?" he asked, ignoring her comment.

"She couldn't take the noise. The place next door is a summer rental and the people throw a lot of parties." She decided against mentioning the halfway house for convicted drug abusers that had recently opened down the block, over the objections of those residents who occupied their own properties. That would only give Mike an opening to point out that it might be handy to have a man with a gun on the premises.

Not *this* man, with or without a gun.

"I don't mind noise," he replied. "I can afford the rent. And I'll bet I could charm the socks off your landlord."

"Why do you say that?"

"Landlords love renting to security experts."

"I'm the landlord," Paige said. "I own the place."

Mike barely blinked before barreling onward. "Tell me about the bedrooms. Better yet, how about a tour?"

The guy's nerve knew no bounds. "Get your own apartment," she snapped. "Preferably a two-bedroom so there'll be room for both of you."

"I know I'll regret asking this but—both of who?"

"You and your ego." She hated letting this man get to her, but the crack about touring the bedrooms was too much.

Instead of answering, he toyed with the slip of paper. She mulled the possibility of snatching it from his hand and decided the effort would be undignified.

Besides, even though he had her phone number, Mike wouldn't dare harass her. If he did, Paige would file a restraining order. Assuming the guy had a concealed-weapon license, he'd be in big trouble.

"You really do think the most interesting things," he observed. "I tried to count the expressions that fleeted across your face but I ran out of fingers."

"While I'd love to stand here discussing my facial contortions, I have patients to see." Actually, she had half an hour to spare and the medical office building was right next door, but it seemed a good excuse to end this conversation.

"See you Saturday," Mike said cheerfully. "Save me a dance."

That surprised her. He hadn't danced with anyone at Nora's wedding, which she'd noticed because she was curious about how such a big guy moved. "I don't think so."

"You don't know how to dance?"

"Of course I do!" She rarely got a chance, though. Too few guys felt comfortable dancing with a woman her height.

"Wear something pretty. People tend to stare when a couple of giants like us take the floor."

"Oh, rats. I was planning to wear scrubs to the wedding," she shot back.

Mike grinned. "Make it a slow dance. I'm sure we'll both enjoy it."

"I haven't said yes."

"It's against the law to blow off the best man." He tucked the paper into his pocket. "See you Saturday." And off he strolled.

Paige felt as if steam might shoot out of her ears. It galled her that he'd gotten the last word. And that, as he well knew, she could hardly snub him in front of friends and colleagues.

Well, what difference did it make if they took a turn around the dance floor? As for moving into her house, he didn't have a prayer.

If the universe was throwing Mike Aaron into Paige's life, the universe had better get over it.

MIKE HAD ENJOYED NEEDLING Paige Brennan ever since the wedding last year, when she'd overheard his casual reference to her as an Amazon and gone ballistic. Didn't she realize that her overreactions made it fun to tease her?

He hadn't been kidding about wanting to rent a room in her house, though. He would enjoy living close to the beach, and he hated apartments. Even beach cottages provided more elbow room.

He was a good roommate. Organized, reliable, healthy. Okay, possibly a touch overbearing, but she could obviously stand up to him. After the cataclysm that had been his marriage, Mike never intended to try *that* again, but he liked female companionship.

He waited for an elevator, which took longer than expected, and reached the ground floor just as the nearby stairwell door wheezed shut behind Paige. Off she strode toward the staff entrance, a tendril of red hair defiantly escaping its pins. He preferred her tresses loose, the way she'd worn them when he'd run into her at the beach. He also preferred her wearing that bikini. A glimpse of her stunning half-naked figure beneath the white coat would be a complete turn-on.

If he and Paige became roommates, Mike hoped he'd see plenty of everything. Much as she protested, he hadn't missed the flare of attraction that dilated her pupils and tightened her body. He'd bet that within a month they'd be sharing not only a house, but also a bed.

Excellent.

Mike refused to worry about another renter appearing before he figured out how to change her mind. To anticipate failure was to invite it.

He glanced at his watch. Just enough time to cross town and arrive at his two o'clock appointment. Kendall Technologies, which developed and manufactured medical devices, contracted with Fact Hunter Investigations to run background checks on its new hires at its facilities in

Safe Harbor and in Phoenix. The work might be routine, but it helped pay the bills. When you owned a company, that counted for a lot.

Strolling through the lobby, Mike let his thoughts drift back to Paige. He'd enjoyed the verbal sparring. With that expressive face, she would be a lousy poker player...or a delightful partner at strip poker.

Thank goodness his teasing had distracted her from asking what he was doing at the hospital. While he'd told his immediate family, he didn't care to broadcast the news that he'd become a sperm donor. Fortunately, his parents had accepted his decision with only a trace of regret.

They understood becoming a sperm donor was a highly personal decision. It was certainly none of Dr. Paige Brennan's concern, future roommate or not.

Chapter Two

Wear something pretty.
No, I'll deliberately choose something ugly.

Paige was glad she hadn't said that. Her crack about wearing scrubs hadn't been especially clever, either. In retrospect, she wished she'd ignored the remark entirely.

Even more, she wished that five-minute conversation with Mike Aaron hadn't kept playing through her mind for the past four days. Now glaring into her closet, she tried to decide what to wear to the wedding. Her wardrobe was divided between pantsuits appropriate for work and supercasual beach clothes. Even before she'd inherited this house six months ago, she'd lived nearby and spent a lot of time here with Aunt Bree.

Her russet cocktail dress was the wrong color for a June wedding. As a last resort, she took out the low-cut green sheath she'd bought for Nora's ceremony and examined it critically. What had possessed her to choose a dress so sexy, revealing the cleft of her breasts and emphasizing the emerald shade of her eyes? She'd be embarrassed if Mike remembered it and made some snippy remark. Or if he stared down her cleavage as he'd done on Tuesday.

No, if he did that, *he* was the one who should be embarrassed.

From next door, the sudden *boom-thumpa-boom* of an

overamped stereo shook her small house. Only two-thirty in the afternoon and those idiot renters were already starting their party. Paige released an impatient breath. Thank goodness she'd be gone most of the day and all night. With luck, this trio of party-hearty young women would be gone by Sunday. She hoped the next set of weekly renters would be more considerate.

Shaking off her annoyance, she examined the tantalizing spill of green fabric. It was flattering and expensive, and she'd only worn it twice, to the wedding and on an internet-arranged date that was best forgotten. Who cared if Mike stared at her?

Paige laid the dress across the bed's blue-and-white quilt and, going to the window, drew the blue print curtains. As she did, a drift of her aunt's lavender perfume brought a rush of nostalgia. Since her parents' deaths five years ago, Paige hadn't felt truly loved by anyone except her elderly aunt. In some ways, even while her mother and father were alive, she'd been closer to Bree.

Other members of the family—including Paige's five much older brothers and sisters—had considered Aunt Brenda disagreeably eccentric. She'd shortened her name to Bree, chosen never to marry and spouted colorful opinions that rubbed her conservative Texas relatives the wrong way. Legend had it that Bree had even been arrested once at an antinuclear protest.

By the time Paige moved to California to attend medical school, Bree was in her seventies and had mellowed from the young firebrand who'd scandalized the family. She'd been supportive and a source of excellent advice. And now she was gone.

Aunt Bree had left Paige this house along with enough money to pay off most of her student loans, but Paige would trade all that to have her back. Tears prickled as she slipped on the dress. She wished Bree were here now, more than ever. To share the low moments and especially the happy ones.

Paige's period still hadn't started. Being almost a week late might not mean anything, since she wasn't always regular. Still, an excited shiver ran through her. As she sat at the dressing table to apply makeup, the mirror showed a face brighter than usual, with freckles slightly darker. Both increased blood flow and increased pigmentation could be signs of early pregnancy. As could the uneasiness in her stomach these past few days.

Eight months from now, she might be bringing home a baby. What a miracle! Yet, although she'd planned for this, Paige could hardly wrap her mind around the reality. Or the potential reality.

Boom-thumpa-boom. The drumbeats after a quiet interval made her hand jerk, smearing her makeup. Muttering in annoyance, Paige wiped her face and started over.

Her thoughts returned to the issue of a roommate. Despite her inheritance, she needed to be careful about finances, and the rent would be welcome, especially since Paige couldn't count on finding anyone to share the house once she bore a child.

She'd received two responses to her ad on the hospital board. A lab tech had stopped by Thursday night with her boyfriend. Incredibly, they'd expected to both move in for the price of one. Then an admitting clerk had called last night, but backed off after an explosion of rap music from next door drowned out the phone conversation.

No word from Mike, thank goodness. Well, someone would come along soon. Summertime at the beach was an irresistible lure.

Makeup complete, Paige put on a pair of earrings made of bright green sea glass. She'd begun collecting the colorful, naturally polished pieces of glass during beach walks with Aunt Bree before her degenerative disease—amyotrophic lateral sclerosis, better known as Lou Gehrig's Disease—deteriorated her health in the final months. They'd both loved the glimmering colors and shapes.

Bree had had these pieces made into earrings and given them to Paige in early December. Aware that her aunt's days were numbered, Paige had prepared a gift of her own: a video slide show of Bree's early years, longtime friends and special moments with Paige. Her aunt had watched it over and over, right up until the morning she died, two days before Christmas. Now Paige had the video to help relive those precious times.

Rising, she smoothed the dress over her hips. Bree had urged her to enjoy life and not dwell on the past. Today, she meant to take that advice.

And since she'd be dancing with a guy taller than she was, she could afford to wear a pair of three-inch heels. Slipping on a shiny black-and-white pair she hadn't been able to resist buying, Paige transferred her wallet and tissues into a coordinating purse.

After running a brush through her shoulder-length auburn hair, she was ready to go. She checked the window locks and the rear door, set the alarm and went out the front, locking the bolt behind her.

Bright sunshine took the edge off the sea breeze as Paige crossed the brick patio with its white rattan furniture and blue-and-white cushions. The rumble of waves from half a block to her left softened the outrageous noise from the right. On the two-lane street, a woman cycled by, a leashed dog pacing alongside. Down the block, a father was playing Frisbee with a pair of energetic boys on the sidewalk.

As Paige clicked open her garage door, the music

paused. Welcome relief—until a shrill wolf whistle split the air. She knew without looking where that came from. Since the halfway house had opened on the next corner, there always seemed to be seedy-looking men hanging around the porch, harassing any woman under fifty who ventured into view.

Paige hurried into the garage. When had it become open season on women around here? While she had sympathy for recovering addicts, many of the residents had been court-ordered into treatment as a condition of their release from prison, according to testimony before the majority of city council members approved a use permit for the facility. She wished those members who'd approved the permit had to live near these men and be subjected to their rudeness.

She slid into the bucket seat of her aging but well-kept blue sports coupe. Time to forget obnoxious neighbors and everything else weighing on her mood.

Paige Brennan planned to have fun. And nobody better get in her way.

"I HAVE THE RING," MIKE MURMURED, patting his tuxedo pocket.

"Of course you have the ring. You're the most anal-retentive...I mean, reliable guy I know," Lock replied from the corner of his mouth, keeping his gaze fixed on the back of the wedding chapel where in a few minutes Erica Benford would appear in all her bridal splendor.

Under normal circumstances, Mike might have considered wrestling his brother to the ground to retaliate for that remark, but not in a wedding chapel. And certainly not in front of their gathered family and friends, along with Erica's relatives who'd flown in from Boston.

Gazing across the shining faces of his parents, his

sister, Marianne, and a couple of grown foster kids who'd become a permanent part of the Aaron family, Mike felt an unaccustomed swell of nostalgia. It had been more than twenty years since a hurt, angry twelve-year-old named Sherlock Vaughn became the latest kid to share Mike's bedroom at their house in the inland city of Pomona.

Lock had run away from his previous foster home, and this was his last chance before assignment to a group care facility. Mike hadn't been crazy about this rough-and-tumble kid with an attitude as big as nearby Mount Baldy.

Gradually, he'd learned that Lock had had a series of bad breaks, being relinquished at birth and adopted by a couple who developed serious drug problems. The adoptive father had abandoned the family and the adoptive mother ended up in prison.

Over the years, Mike and Lock had fought their share of battles, physical and verbal. They'd also become close friends. While they'd attended different colleges, both chose careers in law enforcement. At Mike's wedding half a dozen years ago, Lock had been best man, and now he was returning the favor.

Mike hoped his brother's marriage turned out better than his. He'd told Sheila up front that he didn't want children, but she hadn't believed him. Her resentment had festered until everything fell apart. Mike tried to be philosophical about the mess because the less he thought about it, the better.

In the chapel, the last of the guests settled into their seats. Nearly three o'clock, the designated hour for the ceremony.

Mike surveyed the group from the hospital: Dr. Owen Tartikoff, world-famous head of the fertility program; his wife, Bailey; plus a few others on the surgical team that

Erica worked with. Mike had met most of them before, and made a point of recalling their names.

For an indulgent moment, he allowed his gaze to fix on Paige Brennan, sitting in their midst. He'd been fighting the urge to stare at the striking redhead ever since she entered the chapel in that form-fitting dress. She'd worn her hair loose, the color so rich he ached to sink his hands into it, or better yet spread it across a pillow as he slid down her straps to bare the swell of her breasts.

Mike yanked his attention away. If anyone in this roomful of people noticed his reaction to Paige, he'd never live it down.

Mercifully, the piano changed themes, auguring in the matron of honor in a long dark-pink dress. The sturdy figure and strong, lined face belonged to Lock's birth mother Renée Green, with whom he'd recently reconnected. A hospital volunteer, she'd become friends with Erica as well, and now the prospect of her grandchild's birth had brought her joyously into the family.

The music changed again, and the velvet curtain parted. In sailed a glowing Erica, her white lace gown obscuring the slight thickening at her waist. Her widowed mother, Bernadette, who went by the nickname Bibi, escorted her daughter with pride.

Paige angled in her seat to watch, her lovely face intense with yearning. She seemed riveted by the bride.

Was she longing to walk down the aisle herself, or was the longing aimed at the bride's pregnancy? Maybe both. That didn't mean Mike and the gorgeous lady doc couldn't enjoy some good times, but he'd be careful.

Bibi Benford relinquished her daughter and retreated to a front-row seat. At last night's rehearsal, she'd told Mike how much she enjoyed traveling and shopping with her sisters, relishing the freedom now that her daughter was grown. He understood perfectly because he treasured his freedom after an adolescence spent shepherding whiny kids. That had been enough parenting to last him a lifetime.

No danger of falling prey to some biological imperative. As a sperm donor, he was not only helping childless couples but also leaving his legacy to the next generation. Case closed.

The radiant bride joined the groom at the altar. Lock was grinning so hard Mike wouldn't be surprised if the two of them, after exchanging vows, simply floated off on their honeymoon.

He turned his attention to the minister and prepared to produce the ring.

PAIGE HADN'T EXPECTED the world to suddenly look different. Although she kept trying to rein in her hopes, she felt as if powerful hormones were flooding her system, awakening her to fresh perspectives.

The bride's pregnancy, plus seeing her with her mother, reminded Paige that behind the new family lay thousands of mothers who'd given birth and raised babies over the millennia. Erica—and perhaps Paige—had become part of a chain of life that would stretch into the far-distant future.

Now, in the large reception room, Paige watched the photographer pose the wedding party. Her eye traced the resemblance between Lock and his birth mother, the strong jawline and tilt of the head. Nearby, Erica and her mom formed a matched set with their petite figures and blond hair.

Who would Paige's baby resemble? Her, of course, but there'd be a paternal influence, as well. What unknown chain of men and women lay behind this tiny and still theoretical infant?

She knew some details about the donor from his description in the computer profile. Over six feet tall, with light brown hair and gray eyes, he'd tested as highly stable on the psychological screening. A professional man with a master's degree, he enjoyed excellent health, and three of his grandparents had lived to a gratifyingly old age. One grandmother had suffered from type 2 diabetes, which was usually controllable with diet and exercise.

Yet what did he really look like? Whose smile would she see on her child's face every morning? If her little one had a dimple or odd-shaped toes, she might never know whether they came from the father or from one of her own ancestors. And the child would never know, either.

As the guests found their places at the round tables, Paige spotted her colleague, Dr. Zack Sargent, with his eight-year-old stepdaughter, Berry. He'd told Paige the whole story once while they waited to observe Dr. Tartikoff perform an innovative surgical technique. He'd adopted the little girl when he married her mother, and was raising her alone since his wife had died of heart disease three years ago. His daughter didn't resemble him— her mother had been African-American—but there was no mistaking the love flowing between them.

Paige and her child would share that same kind of unshakable love. And that was what counted.

Still, life was never that simple. Having grown up with five bossy siblings, Paige had figured being a family of two would be luxuriously intimate. Now doubts began creeping in. Didn't a child deserve to know both parents? What about unsuspected medical issues that might not have shown up since the father hadn't yet reached middle age? And while Paige had chafed at her siblings' attempts to control her, her own child might long for a brother or sister.

Her gaze fixed on Mike, who was posing with the bride and groom, along with several young people and an older couple who must be the Aarons. According to Erica, Mike had flourished in a family enlarged by foster kids. He certainly looked in high spirits next to a woman only a few inches shorter than him, identical sandy hair tickling the collar of her dress. On his other side, he looped an arm around a shorter woman whose high cheekbones and dark coloring indicated a Hispanic and perhaps part Native American heritage. What a warm, stimulating household he'd grown up in.

In the abstract, compensating for the absence of a dad hadn't struck her as all that difficult. But regarding Mike's tall, steady figure, she wondered how exactly she was going to do that.

Well, a woman shouldn't be denied motherhood simply because she'd given up on finding the right man. Lots of mothers raised their families alone and Paige could, too.

"You're sitting with us!" The cheerful greeting from Dr. Nora Franco roused Paige.

"Wonderful." She turned to greet Nora's husband, Leo, a police detective who'd once worked with Mike. "I hope they're going to serve food soon," Paige added as the three of them took seats.

"Did you skip lunch?"

On the point of answering that she'd eaten a sandwich but her stomach was churning, Paige realized how revealing that comment would be. Not only had Nora known Paige since they'd served their residencies together, she was also an obstetrician. She might notice the possible sign of early pregnancy.

"Something like that." Quickly, Paige changed the subject. "Any idea when you're coming back to work? Not that I'm in a hurry." Eager to join the Safe Harbor staff, Paige had taken over Nora's practice during her maternity leave.

"I hate to tear myself away from Neo. He's incredibly cute, and I had no idea a seven-month-old could be so smart." Nora chuckled. "Just listen to me! Anyway, when I do, I'd prefer to work part-time, so I hope you'll stay on."

"That sounds great." It was exactly what Paige wanted. She was enjoying the patients, and the chance to advance her surgical skills and learn the newest fertility treatments. With her previous medical group, she'd felt her skills stagnating. She'd had personal reasons for leaving, as well.

Her attention shifted to the bridal table, where Erica and Lock sat among a flock of relatives. "Do you ever miss being part of a big family?" she blurted. Nora's only close relative was a father who lived several hours' drive away. "I mean, now that you have a baby."

"Leo's brother Tony lives close by," her friend reminded her. "And my sister-in-law Kate's been very helpful. Neo loves playing with his cousins."

"Cousins are great," Paige replied automatically, and recalled with a pang that her baby wouldn't grow up anywhere near his or her cousins. In fact, thanks to the ten-year age difference between her and the youngest of her siblings, Paige's nieces and nephews ranged from school age up to their late twenties.

Still, a couple of her nieces and nephews had babies of their own. *Maybe we wouldn't be so isolated, after all.*

"You're thinking again." The amused baritone belonged to Mike. With a fluid motion, he reversed the empty chair beside Paige and straddled it. "Someone ought to make a video of your face and put it on YouTube. It would go viral."

Paige shuddered. "Don't talk to a doctor about going viral. It raises scary associations."

Nora cast a knowing look in their direction and, after congratulating Mike on his brother's wedding, turned her attention to Zack and his daughter on her far side. Paige couldn't blame her for assuming they were indulging in a flirtation.

"Speaking of viral, that dress could give a guy a fever," Mike joked.

Oh, for heaven's sake! "Aren't you supposed to sit with the bride and groom?" Paige asked testily.

"Are you avoiding the subject?"

"You mean the subject of my voluptuous body?" Might as well give him a direct answer. "Yes, because it's none of your business."

"Then why aren't you all covered up like my sister Marianne?"

Maybe it was the teasing light in those blue-gray eyes, or the inviting glint of white teeth. Most likely, she was feeling the contrary effects of hormones. Whatever the cause, Paige found herself wishing that she could have a real conversation with Mike Aaron that didn't involve innuendo.

"You must like me or you wouldn't keep showing up in my path," she said. "So let me give you a tip, Mike. I guess it's a cliché to say women don't like being treated as sex objects, and maybe some do, but not me. Talk to me with respect. Treat me like a friend. I'm not saying that'll get you anywhere, but it won't make me dread dancing with you."

He started to speak and hesitated. She could practically see the gears shifting.

"It's fun to tease you. You flush bright red and I guess I enjoy the reaction," Mike admitted.

"Well, I *don't* enjoy it."

"What else should we talk about?"

Paige chose the first topic that came to mind. "How about what it's like to grow up in a big family."

"Chaotic," he said.

"For me, it was claustrophobic."

"How many siblings do you have?" he asked.

"Three brothers and two sisters. All much older." The senior brother, Curren, a radiologist, had recently turned fifty-three.

"I assumed you had at most one sibling," Mike said.

"Why is that?"

"It must take a lot of encouragement and support to go to med school." As he spoke, he seemed like a different guy, straightforward and thoughtful. Not that Paige expected this new attitude to last, but it was an appealing change.

"My family opposed my career plans, even though my dad was a doctor and so are two of my brothers," she said. "They thought I should be a nurse like my mom and sisters and take time out to raise a family. Also, they weren't convinced that I could hack it. To them, I'm the baby."

"A big and very luscious baby," came the immediate response, followed by, "Sorry. Force of habit."

The way he ducked his head was endearing. Paige felt an unexpected touch of regret when she saw Lock waving from the head table. "They're signaling you over there."

Mike glanced toward his brother. "Ah. Duty calls." He patted his pocket. "I've got my toast all prepared."

"That comes later, I'm sure. Right now it looks like the food's ready." Wait staff had begun setting salads in front of the bridal party.

"See you when the music starts." Flashing a grin, Mike uncoiled from the chair and cut away between tables.

She was rather looking forward to that dance, Paige discovered. And that was the most surprising thing of all.

Chapter Three

Mike could see he had to plan his campaign differently. Flirting and teasing came naturally to him, but he hadn't meant to offend Paige.

Her frankness impressed him. She was smart and assertive, and interesting to talk to. He also liked that, while she was obviously capable of taking care of herself, she'd shown a sweet, vulnerable side when she mentioned her family's lack of encouragement.

Contrary to the impression he'd apparently given, he didn't consider her simply a sex object. Mike had no interest in shallow relationships. On the other hand, he had no interest in falling in love and getting his comfortable life torn to shreds, either.

The fact that he genuinely liked Paige made this dangerous territory. If anyone could tempt his emotions to venture too far, it might be her. But what fun was life without a little risk? As for her feelings, he intended to lay his cards on the table, so there'd be no misunderstandings.

They were both grown-ups. And neither of them could deny the attraction that had flared from the moment they met. Now Mike understood why his occasional overtures since then hadn't lit any fires. He'd gone about this the wrong way.

Thank goodness she'd set him on the right track. Now he just had to figure out how to persuade her—in a friendly, respectful manner—to let him move into her house. And become her lover.

He really did need a place to live. As he finished his toast and watched Lock and Erica entwine arms to sip champagne, Mike had to admit he'd be glad to move out, and the sooner the better. Wedding gifts covered the pool table and crowded the kitchen counter. Baby gear filled the living room and made it hard to have his buddies over to watch TV. As for the refrigerator, he had a hard time finding space.

The meal and the toasts flew by, and across the room the band began warming up. Soon the leader was calling for the bridal couple to kick off the first dance.

"You should have practiced," Mike told Lock.

"I know how to dance." His brother sprang to his feet and helped Erica up.

"You never—" Mike broke off. His brother had avoided dancing in high school, but they hadn't seen much of each other in the intervening years until Lock moved back from Arizona the previous summer. He wasn't sure why he'd assumed the guy still didn't dance. After all, most people figured Mike didn't, either.

"Never what?" Lock demanded.

"Never mind," he said, and was rewarded by a chuckle from his brother.

"Just watch my toes." The petite nurse took her husband's arm. "These shoes are fragile. Not to mention my feet." She'd obviously noticed that Lock tended to make up in energy what he lacked in grace.

"I'll be careful."

A guy who was five feet ten could get away with winging it on the dance floor, Mike mused as he watched them make their way between tables. When you towered over people, everyone noticed your stumbles. Mike had taken ballroom lessons because he hated making a fool of himself. He was glad now. While he might be a little rusty, he remembered most of the moves.

The guests called out appreciatively as the tiny bride and her muscular husband swept around the floor in a waltz. Soon the senior Aarons joined them. Mike's father, Joe, held himself tall and straight and gazed lovingly down at his wife, clearly still enraptured.

What was it like to spend thirty-five years together, raising two children of your own along with foster kids who numbered well into the double digits? Hadn't his father ever longed for peace and quiet after a hard day drilling teeth and filling cavities? Mike wondered. And as a kindergarten teacher, his mother ought to have had her fill of kids at school. Yet they'd welcomed each new child with enthusiasm.

When Mike came home from the office, he liked having his pick of activities. A game of pool, a session on his treadmill, an evening with the guys. Still, there *was* something he'd like to add to the list. It involved a stunning redhead with a smart mouth and a determined tilt to her chin.

Across the floor, Paige was still eating. No sense trying to drag her away from her meal. Mike preferred to wait and approach in a laid-back manner in keeping with their new entente.

Instead, he addressed the bride's mother, sitting across the table. "Bibi, would you do me the honor of a dance?"

"I'd be delighted." The trim, well-dressed blonde, who looked too young to have a thirty-one-year-old daughter, rose gracefully.

He hadn't considered the difference in their heights,

Mike realized as he and Bibi circled the dance floor. People were grinning at the sight of them, but if she didn't mind, neither did he. All the same, he was glad when one of the hospital staffers cut in.

Mike was about to ask Paige to dance when he felt the phone vibrating in his pocket. It was the answering service, he noted on the readout, and retreated to a hallway. "What's up?"

"A woman called and said it was urgent," came the familiar voice of Naomi Arrigo, who owned the service. "She identified herself as Mrs. Jones."

"I don't recognize the name." If that was even her real name.

"She said she's new. But very anxious to get hold of you." Naomi had a list of instructions to follow when calls came in, including asking whether the person was a current client.

Mike saw no reason to interrupt his brother's wedding reception for an appointment that could most likely wait. Still, he didn't like to ignore a potentially serious situation. "Did she describe the nature of her business?"

"Only that it's personal."

If the woman was being threatened or beaten, she should call the police. But some women refused to notify the authorities even in the face of abuse. "How upset was she?"

"She was breathing hard, almost hyperventilating," Naomi reported. "But she calmed down after we talked for a minute. I asked if she's in danger and she said no, and then she insisted I contact you to make sure you'll see her first thing Monday morning. She sounded like someone who's used to being obeyed."

Mike consulted his digital calendar. Although he had a busy week ahead with Lock gone, he'd been careful not to overbook. "I'll slot her for 10 a.m. Monday. Where would she like to meet?" Depending on the nature of their problem, clients might prefer his office, their own premises or a neutral site such as a restaurant.

"Let me put you on hold and I'll get right back to you," the operator replied.

He passed the next couple of minutes reviewing his schedule and listening to a rock number emanating from the reception. Naomi wasted no time picking up again. "Ten o'clock is fine. At first she mentioned her home, but then she decided you might be spotted, so I gave her directions to the office. Sorry. That's probably more information than you needed."

"There's no such thing," Mike corrected. "One mysterious Mrs. Jones on the docket for 10 a.m. Monday. Thanks."

"Glad to help, Mr. Aaron."

As he reentered the large room, the music segued into a cha-cha. Although fast, it required the couple to hold each other, which was a definite plus. Mike didn't see the point of dancing without physical contact.

Oh, now, hold on. A fancy dance like this discouraged most participants, but a fellow with russet hair a shade brighter than Paige's was already leading her onto the dance floor. It was none other than Dr. Tartikoff, who was more or less her boss at the hospital. Happily married, too, judging by the way his wife nodded approvingly from the sidelines. So nothing to worry about.

Except that Mike didn't like getting beaten to the punch. Or the fluid way the two doctors went through their paces, hips shifting, footwork crisp, almost as if they'd rehearsed. Dr. Tartikoff might be slightly shorter than his partner, but his effortless confidence made him seem taller. An alpha male, without a doubt. The kind who considered that all the women in his sphere belonged to him.

Mike tamped down his instinctive competitiveness. The doc wasn't trying to pick up Paige right in front of his wife. And the women of Safe Harbor Medical Center didn't constitute a harem, either. Look at Erica, Dr. T's favorite surgical nurse, getting married right under his nose.

That might be why he was asserting his masculinity in full view of everyone. And doing a damn fine job of it, Mike had to admit as other dancers dropped away to watch. But who could pay attention to Dr. T when Paige looked so spectacular? The green dress caressed her curves, her eyes shone and her entire body moved in synch with the beat.

Mike should be the man partnering her. He wanted that gleaming smile to focus on him. *Yes, but it's fun being able to stand back and watch her, too.*

At last the song ended. When the pair finished with a flourish, applause erupted across the room.

Paige's partner escorted her off the floor. Stepping forward, Mike smoothly took her elbow. "Great job," he told them.

"Thanks." Dr. T gave a nod of acknowledgment before departing toward his table.

"That was possessive of you," Paige murmured. She didn't sound irked, just breathless.

"Ready for another go?" Mike asked. "Or do you need a break?"

The band eased into a slow number. "I'm ready. I prefer to cool down in motion, like a racehorse."

It was an apt comparison, with her long legs and sleek lines. "Where'd you learn to cha-cha like that?"

"I took dance classes in high school." She kept hold of

Mike's arm as they made their way to the rapidly filling dance area. "And the occasional refresher course."

"You're very coordinated." Not the most graceful compliment to pay a woman, but genuine.

"I'd better be. I'm a surgeon."

"Hand-eye coordination is different."

"Surgery also requires kinesthetic awareness and stamina."

"How's that?" Mike asked as he rested one hand on the lady's tantalizingly nipped-in waist and enfolded her hand in his. He'd never considered that surgery had much in common with athletics.

"Operations can last for hours. Delivering babies takes strength, too. And you have to be alert at any hour, even when roused from a deep sleep. Babies don't wait for the alarm clock to ring." Her cheerful tone made her job sound like a treat. The energy radiating from her was downright sexy.

"I'll bet anyone who gets close to you needs stamina, too," he said, and regretted it when he felt her stiffen. "Forget I said that, would you?"

"Consider it done."

He really did have to curb his teasing, Mike reflected. Also, it took concentration to navigate the crowded floor.

He didn't often dance with a woman tall enough to fit against him, her legs easily matching his steps, her lips nearly level with his. Mike resisted the temptation to hold her tighter, and was glad to feel her relaxing.

Casting about for a neutral subject, he said, "Glad to see you and your boss get along."

"He's not exactly my boss and we don't always get along," Paige returned ruefully.

"You don't?" Mike asked, more because he enjoyed

hearing Paige's throaty voice close to his ear than because of any interest in Dr. T.

"It's complicated," she said. "Many of my patients have nothing to do with the fertility program. But I am part of the hospital staff when it comes to performing surgery and using their labs."

"And in that area, Dr. Tartikoff makes the rules?"

"Yes. Subject to the supervision of the hospital administrator, Dr. Rayburn." She indicated a black-haired man built like a quarterback, dancing with a sharp-featured blonde.

"You get along with him?" Mike, who made it a point to get to know community leaders, had run into Dr. Rayburn a few times and found him both straightforward and a good listener.

"I'd better. He's my personal doctor, as well as the chief."

"How can he do both?"

"Like I said, doctors have stamina," Paige replied brightly.

"So do detectives," Mike mused.

"Don't you focus on administrative duties? I mean, as the owner."

"Co-owner, with Lock. He and Patty, our other agent, handle most of the fieldwork, while I take care of the administration and bringing in new business. I also specialize in online research, but I like to keep active."

"Aren't you the boss?" she asked.

"I try to order Lock around, but he's not buying it. Patty's no pushover, either."

She sniffed. "I had the impression you like being in control."

Much as Mike wanted to argue, he couldn't. "True. But

that doesn't mean I always get my wish." Out of curiosity, he added, "You don't like bossy men, do you?"

"Not usually."

At least she'd qualified her remark, Mike reflected. "What type of men *do* you prefer? If they're too easygoing, surely they'd bore the socks off you."

Several moments passed while she considered. The music shifted into a faster tempo, and he was concerned he might lose her. But she merely adjusted her stride to his as they twirled faster.

"Men I respect," Paige said at last. "How about you— what's your type? Cute little ladies, or Amazons like me?"

Mike ignored the teasing reminder of his reference to her. "I don't think I have a type. My ex-wife was short."

"That's it? Short?"

"Flirtatious."

"Assertive?" Paige offered.

"More…passive-aggressive." *The type who punishes her husband for not wanting kids by having an affair. And then marrying the guy she cheated with.* "And unfaithful, but let's not go into that."

She took in the information thoughtfully. "How long have you been divorced, if you don't mind my asking?"

"It's been final for two years." While they were on the subject, might as well satisfy his curiosity. While he *could* access public records, Mike preferred not to snoop on his friends. "You ever been married?"

"Nope," she said.

"Engaged?"

"Not even close." Paige halted so abruptly he nearly stumbled.

"What's wrong?" He hadn't meant to broach a touchy subject.

"I felt dizzy. Sorry."

"Too much exercise right after eating." She did look pale beneath the dusting of freckles. As Mike guided her off the dance floor, he felt an urge to protect her, the way he'd once protected his younger siblings. "It's not as if we have a shortage of doctors around. Want me to fetch one?"

"Once I sit down, I'll be fine."

Empty places at her table indicated her friends must be dancing or off visiting. "I'll wait here with you."

Catching her dubious expression, Mike supposed he should have asked permission rather than making a statement. The hell with that. He was a pushy guy, and there was only so much he could do about it.

For whatever reason, she didn't argue. As she sank into her chair, he hoped this didn't mean she was truly feeling unwell.

Drawing out a chair for himself, Mike observed that, at the head table, his parents were taking note of his attentions to Paige. So, no doubt, was the rest of the family. But he'd taught them long ago not to pester him about his private life.

The music stopped. Amid a smattering of applause for the band, the leader said, "I've been informed that the bride and groom are about to cut the cake. It's spice cake, in case anyone's wondering, so don't miss out!"

"Would you like some?" Mike asked Paige.

"Thank you. I would." She gave him a wan smile.

He rose, glad for something to do. "Maybe a sugar rush will help that famous stamina kick in."

"It had better. I'm on call tonight." She waved a dismissive hand. "It's already passing, whatever it was."

"Great." But as Mike headed toward the table where Erica and Lock were doing the honors, he wondered if Paige might be hiding something.

That was the trouble with being a detective. You tended to get suspicious about everything.

PAIGE HADN'T EXPECTED the hormones to hit this hard, this early. While that didn't guarantee she was pregnant, she resolved to administer a test at the first chance.

If she was pregnant, dramatic changes were taking place right now inside her body. The baby might be a millimeter long and its tiny nervous system, bones, blood and other organs were developing as layers of cells. Unfortunately, thinking about that didn't help her queasiness.

From the far side of the room, she caught Dr. Mark Rayburn's concerned glance. He knew about her artificial insemination, since he'd performed it. Luckily, his wife, Dr. Samantha Forrest, spoke to him and drew his attention away. Much as Paige liked Mark, she was in no mood for fatherly intervention.

She glanced toward the cake line. While she couldn't see the bridal couple through the crowd, she did have a great view of Mike's commanding head and shoulders rising above the other guests. A shiver of pleasure ran through her at the memory of his hand on her waist and his cheek brushing hers.

She was impressed by the way he'd taken her rebuke to heart. He seemed genuinely concerned about her well-being. And now that he'd dropped the annoying jokes, they'd talked easily, skimming across subjects, leaving her hungry for more. More conversation, and more of his touch.

I like him. Not much of a revelation, Paige supposed, but until today she hadn't considered Mike a guy she wanted to date, let alone anything more.

Before deciding to have a baby alone, she'd ruled out any likelihood of meeting a suitable man. Her aunt's death, followed closely by Paige's thirty-fourth birthday, had made her keenly aware of time passing. Delivering babies and being surrounded by pregnant women had stoked her longing, while observing the struggles of fertility patients reminded her that, despite modern technology, women had a relatively narrow window of opportunity for conceiving.

What rotten timing to discover, just when she might have reached the next step of her journey, that Mike had a likable side. Contrary to the way she usually thought of herself, she was enjoying his protectiveness. Was pregnancy awakening some susceptibility, a primal yearning to depend on male support? Paige bit her lip at the troubling notion.

Her sister Juno would lecture that she should have waited until she found a husband. Maeve would counter that things were unfolding this way for a reason. Funny how, even though Paige rarely talked to her sisters, she still heard their voices in her head.

She pushed away her distressing thoughts. One dance with Mike fell far short of a long-term relationship. In any case, she wasn't about to rethink her decision. If she were lucky enough to have a baby, she'd be forever grateful.

A child was so much more than just a cute little infant. Parenthood meant bringing a whole person into the world, nurturing him or her, and becoming part of a vast ongoing experience. It meant offering a gift to the future, to that child's spouse and their own children and everyone their lives would touch. It was a tremendous responsibility and a blessing beyond measure.

Still, Paige had no illusions about how a guy was likely to react to the news that she was bearing someone else's baby, especially a macho guy like Mike. Thank goodness she'd refused to rent to him. After today, she'd make excuses to avoid his company. Any further contact could only lead to discomfort and awkwardness.

Anyway, once the first flush of pregnancy passed, Paige expected to recover her resilience. Mind and body would normalize. She'd do fine on her own.

In her purse, her cell rang. Although her 12-hour on-call shift didn't start until 8 p.m., she'd left a standing request to be notified when any of her own patients went into labor. But instead of the familiar hospital designation, the display said Security.

Why was her alarm company calling?

Mike returned, sliding a plate of cake in front of her. After mouthing, "thanks," Paige answered the call. "Dr. Brennan."

"This is Safe Harbor Security," said a young male voice. "May I have your code, please, Dr. Brennan?"

That was a safety precaution in case someone else answered her phone. "Glimmerglass." Usually she didn't like for anyone else to hear, but she considered Mike trustworthy.

"Dr. Brennan, an alarm's gone off at your house," the man said. "Are you at home now?"

"No. Please call the police."

"Right away. Excuse me." She could hear him telling someone else to make the call, and then he returned to the line. "My associate is doing that now."

"Which window?" Paige asked. The kitchen window rattled when large trucks passed, although so far never hard enough to activate an alarm.

"It's the window in the rear door."

That gave her a bad feeling. The door, which led directly into the bathroom, opened onto a small courtyard off an alley. She considered it the most tempting point of entry for a would-be burglar. "I'll go home immediately."

"Please use caution," the man warned. "Don't approach the house until the police arrive."

"If someone's broken into my place…" She halted, fighting her distress. "You're right. I'll be careful."

Paige cut off and collected her purse. At Mike's question, she explained the situation tersely, concluding with, "I have to go." Before leaving, though, she took a bite of the cake for good measure. Delicious.

"I'll come with you." Mike stood as she did.

"Thanks, but I'm not dizzy anymore. I can drive just fine." Adrenaline had cleared away the last of her cobwebs.

"I'll follow. I'm an ex-cop, remember? Let me take a look around."

She didn't want Mike anywhere near her house, especially while she was in a vulnerable state. Besides, she remembered something Erica had said about how she and Lock first connected. After he witnessed her narrowly escape being hit by a car, he'd driven her home and stayed to comfort her. One thing had quickly led to another.

Paige refused to let that happen with Mike. "I'm fine."

"You're not arguing me out of this one," he replied firmly. "Even if you never speak to me again, I'm not going to risk having you stumble into an intruder."

"I'm sure the police will be there before me." Response times in this small town ran less than five minutes, Paige had heard.

"It never hurts to have somebody in your corner," Mike returned. "Trust me. There's nothing routine about a burglary."

About to object, she remembered the halfway house. While her first concern had been theft and damage, what if she was the intruder's real target? He might be watching from down the block. He'd see the police depart and know she was left with a broken window in her rear door.

As Mike had said, it wouldn't hurt to have someone in her corner. Right now, depending on a guy didn't seem like such a bad idea. And unlike Erica, she wasn't going to collapse in the man's arms.

"Okay. Thanks," Paige said, and went to take a hurried leave of the bride and groom.

Chapter Four

How ironic that Mike had been trying to finagle an excuse for visiting Paige's home, and now he was simply worried about her. This invasion of her property might make her angry enough to stalk inside and confront a burglar, and while the police usually responded quickly, they could be delayed.

He intended to be there, just in case. Nothing more.

In her shiny blue coupe, she made quite a picture driving along Harbor Bluff Drive with her rich auburn hair drifting around her shoulders, Mike noted through the windshield of his late-model silver sedan. If she opened that sunroof, her hair would whip around like a firestorm. Today, though, she was clearly too intent to bother.

A woman living alone in a small town like Safe Harbor ought to be secure in her own home, but Mike knew better. The beach attracted all kinds of characters. Also, from working crimes against persons at the police department, he'd seen behind the fancy closed doors and elegant drawn curtains. Domestic violence, robbery, sex crimes, even the rare but deeply disturbing homicide troubled the peace of the community. Now, whenever he got bored tracking runaway kids, spying on unfaithful spouses or nailing employees who lied about their credentials, he reminded himself of how much sordidness he was spared.

He certainly didn't want to see a woman he cared about face off against some thug who existed in an entirely different universe. She had no idea how unprepared she was or what such a man might be capable of.

Yet as he followed Paige to the narrow beachfront Seaside Lane, Mike reminded himself not to underestimate her. Doctors spent part of their training in emergency rooms. She wouldn't panic easily.

Interesting woman. He'd enjoyed more discussions about her work and a lot of other topics. During their dance, they'd barely scratched the surface. He'd become caught up in their conversation, despite his instinctive response to the sway of her hips and knowing curve of her mouth.

Dangerous territory, as he already knew. And getting riskier to his heart by the minute. More enticing, too.

Traffic was heavy along the beach route on a Saturday, with visitors prowling in search of parking spots. When he trailed Paige's car onto one of the small residential streets at right angles to the beach road, Mike didn't see a single open space by the curb. Instead, his eye flew to a police car, light bar flashing, double-parked in front of a tan cottage with blue shutters.

Paige's coupe pulled into the driveway and she leaned out to speak to a uniformed patrolman. Mike recognized Bill Sanchez, and a moment later, around the corner of the house, appeared Bill's partner, George Granger.

Mike didn't hear an alarm, so the security company must have shut it off. He wasn't sure how audible it would have been anyway, given the rock music throbbing from the neighbor's house. Guests in cutoffs and swimsuits wandered through the open door and jammed the postage-stamp front yard to stare at the policemen.

When he lowered his window, Mike could smell beer, along with barbecue smoke.

The garage door rolled open. Bill peered inside, then waved Paige in. The officers stood aside as Mike parked in the driveway.

"Friend of yours?" George called as Mike got out. "Hey, I like the monkey suit."

"Penguin suit," Mike corrected, and tossed the tuxedo jacket across his rear seat. "We were at my brother's wedding. You've met Lock." George and Bill had played pool with them a time or two. "I wanted to be sure she wasn't walking into a bad situation."

"More obnoxious than dangerous." Bill indicated the party next door. "We were about to go tell them to turn it down."

Paige emerged from the garage, her expression anxious. In contrast to the half-clad guests next door, she shone like a goddess in her emerald gown. "Did someone get inside?" she asked George, half shouting over the music.

He dragged his gaze from her striking figure. "Someone smashed a rear window but couldn't get the door open. Smart lady, having a double-keyed lock." That meant someone reaching inside couldn't turn the knob without a key. "Judging from the fact that he took a leak on the back steps, I'm guessing he wanted to use the bathroom."

Paige's nose wrinkled. "Gross."

"Hang on." Bill vaulted a low dividing wall and vanished into the next house. A moment later, the music cut off.

"That's a relief," Mike said as he, George and Paige moved to her brick patio. A low-growing acacia screened it on one side, while a white wrought-iron fence discouraged sidewalk trespassers. From a window box spilled striped red petunias, a bright punctuation to the blue-and-white furniture. "Are your neighbors often this noisy?"

"Unfortunately, yes." Paige folded her arms protectively. "There's also a halfway house down the street that has a lot of men hanging around. Things were different when my aunt bought this place in the '60s."

Bill returned with a long-haired blond guy in his early twenties. So drunk he kept stumbling, the fellow had a couple of bandages stuck across a gash on his arm.

At the sight of Paige, the man muttered, "Wow. You with anybody? 'Cause I'm free."

Mike fought down a laugh. Not a funny situation, but the guy was so wasted he had no idea how preposterous his statement was. Paige appeared torn between revulsion and disbelief.

"If you have a dire need to throw up or relieve yourself, better speak now, because you're about to take a ride in the squad car and I don't take kindly to messes," Bill informed him.

"Hey! I told you the truth," the guy protested.

"You sure did. That's why you're under arrest." Bill took out his handcuffs.

"Don't you have to run a DNA test or something?" The man stuck out his chin defiantly.

"You admitted breaking and attempting to enter," Bill replied calmly.

"You haven't read me my rights!" This guy watched too much TV, Mike reflected.

"You confessed of your own free will," Bill answered. "But if it makes you feel better, you have the right to remain silent…" The Miranda warning continued as Bill cuffed the perp.

To Paige, George said, "If it's all right with you, Dr.

Brennan, let's go inside and check around to be sure nothing else was damaged."

She swallowed. "Yes, of course."

"She's a doctor?" the suspect asked as Bill hustled him toward the car. "How about bandaging my arm?"

"How about shutting your mouth?" Bill responded, and folded the squawking guy into the screened-off rear seat.

Mike accompanied Paige and George inside. With its broad windows and red, white and blue theme, the living room felt like an extension of the patio. On the walls, shadow boxes filled with polished sea glass alternated with airy watercolors of sailboats. To the right, the room opened into a small kitchen, with a greenhouse window over the sink.

"Okay so far," Paige said with a quaver, and led them across a hallway and into a red-tiled bathroom. Glass shards littered the floor, and Mike could feel a sea breeze seeping through the spiderwebbed crack in a windowed door. Outside, a few steps led down to a courtyard barely large enough to hold a couple of trash cans. Beyond it lay a narrow alley.

Paige blinked hard. "I know he didn't get in, but it's upsetting."

"You feel violated," Mike suggested. "That's natural."

"I figured it was convenient, being able to enter directly into the bathroom when I was covered in sand." Paige gulped. "Now it seems so exposed."

"It's a good thing you have an alarm." At the top of the window, the small sensor box remained in place. If not for that, she'd have returned home alone, possibly at night, and received a shock. No telling what the guy might have done, or who else might have followed him inside.

"I'd like to check the bedroom windows," the patrolman said.

"Of course." Paige showed them into a charming, old-fashioned bedroom where her delicious, light fragrance enfolded Mike. He could picture Paige wrapping her long legs around him as they sank onto that queen-size quilt.

Down, boy.

Opening the curtains, George surveyed the windowsill. "Doesn't appear disturbed."

"Why would it be?" she asked.

"When he couldn't get through the door, he might have tried somewhere else."

Paige shivered. "The guest room's over here." She escorted them past the bathroom to a slightly smaller chamber. Here, someone had decorated in a more formal style: dark, high-poster bed, lace coverlet and a bureau with small drawers. "All clear in here, too," George said after examining the windows.

"What happens now?" Paige asked as they returned to the living room.

"We'll take him in to sober up. I expect he'll face misdemeanor charges, especially if he's willing to pay restitution."

"I won't have to deal with him myself, will I?"

"Most likely he'll pay through the court," George assured her.

"I've got a coverall in my trunk." Mike always carried several changes of clothing. "If it's okay, I'll put it on and hose off your rear steps."

Paige shot him a warm look. "I would be grateful."

"If you can't get somebody out to replace the glass on a Saturday night, I recommend boarding that up," George added.

"I can take care of it." Mike kept a tool kit handy. "Unless you'd rather do it yourself." He didn't underestimate Paige's home repair skills. Being a surgeon, she could no doubt handle tools as well as he could.

"I'm not sure I can run to the store and finish before I go on call at eight," Paige said. "Mike, I appreciate this..."

"...but that doesn't mean you want to rent me a room," he said. "Believe me, there are no strings attached."

"That room's for rent?" George piped up.

"You already have a roommate," Mike growled. The two partners had once hosted a barbecue at the rental they shared.

"Calm down. I meant for one of the women at the station." The patrolman grinned. "But I can take a hint."

Mike wished he'd kept his big mouth shut. Now his former coworkers would be making jokes at his expense. Well, since they involved a knockout of a lady, that wasn't entirely bad.

Paige shivered as they went outside. "I keep thinking, what if he'd gotten inside?"

"You might have found him asleep in bed like Goldilocks," George replied. "Only a whole lot uglier."

The remark startled a chuckle from Paige. "I guess there is a funny side to this."

In the squad car, the perp sagged against the rear door, while on the nearby lawn guests stood around drinking and regarding the scene as if it had been staged for their entertainment.

"They'll crank up the music as soon as the cruiser leaves," Paige muttered, observing the scene from the patio.

"Want me to make sure they don't?" Mike asked.

Her neck and shoulders relaxed, as if taking comfort from his offer. "Thanks, but you're doing more than enough as it is."

"Okay. I'd better get started." He calculated the tasks

ahead. Wash the steps, measure the broken window and swing by the home improvement store. En route, he'd stop at home, change into jeans and hang up the tuxedo so it didn't sustain damage.

After a moment's hesitation, Paige went inside and returned with a key. "In case I have to go out, just let yourself in. I'll reset the alarm. The code number is 6543."

Mike slipped the key into his pocket. "Any special meaning?" He was good at recalling numbers, but a hint would cement the memory.

"I started with the number of kids in my family and worked down from there. Not very imaginative."

"Better than using your birth date like a lot of people do." A burglar could easily get that information from the internet or by stealing mail.

Next door, the music resumed at a less ear-splitting level. Someone had gotten the message, Mike reflected with satisfaction.

So here he stood on Paige's patio with her key in his pocket, watching the police car head down the street. It was, Mike couldn't help thinking, the perfect opportunity to persuade her to rent to him.

Earlier, she'd objected to his manipulative remarks, and once she recovered her equanimity, she'd resent him for taking advantage of her misfortune. Relationships worked better with a bit of space, anyway. "Listen," Mike said. "You were right about not wanting me to move in."

Her mouth quirked. "I was?"

"For starters, I've got my own furniture and a treadmill." While no doubt he could figure out a way around that, her furnishings did pose an obstacle.

"Oh! That stuff belonged to my aunt Bree's longtime roommate, who died four years ago."

"This is your aunt's house? I thought you owned it."

"I do. She died a few days before Christmas and left it to me." Paige shaded her eyes against the lowering sun. "I was planning to sell the extra furniture to an antiques store if my new roommate didn't need it. I wouldn't mind getting rid of it sooner rather than later."

"Does that mean you've changed your mind about renting to me?" Mike couldn't resist asking.

She gazed at him uncertainly. "I..."

He shook his head. "Never mind. Like I said, you were right the first time. We're getting along, and I'd like us to keep on getting along. But if you're still feeling off balance, I could stay over tonight. By tomorrow you should feel back to normal, and hopefully your neighbors will be too hungover to pester you."

Relief showed on her face. "Thanks. Actually, they're moving out tomorrow, but since there's no connecting door from the garage into the house, I have to walk outside. I won't be coming home until morning, but..."

"No explanations necessary." Best to get his chores under way, Mike decided. The longer they stood here talking, the more aware he became of her soft lips and her chest rising and falling beneath the form-fitting dress. "I'll get to work."

She took a deep breath, which had a spectacular effect on her cleavage and on his nervous system. "Make yourself at home. I'll put sheets on the spare bed."

"Don't bother. I can pick up my bedroll and camp out on the couch. The bed's kind of short for me anyway." Now, Paige's bed would suit him much better. *There you go again.*

This mister-nice-guy approach was driving Mike crazy. Thank goodness he only had to keep it up until tomorrow.

"Okay, then. After I change, I'll clean up the glass," Paige told him.

"Sounds like a plan."

She disappeared inside the house, where she was about to strip off her tantalizing gown. It didn't take much imagination to picture a lacy bra straining over those lovely breasts, and her bare navel inviting his hands to close around her slender waist.

Mike groaned. It was going to be a long night.

Chapter Five

At the hospital that night, when she wasn't checking on a patient or delivering a baby, Paige couldn't stop thinking about Mike sleeping over at her house. Maybe it had been a mistake to accept his offer. Yet the prospect of him standing guard calmed the jitters that started up every time a beeper went off or a loud page came over the intercom. She'd never imagined she would react so powerfully to a simple broken window. Especially considering that the perpetrator had been caught.

During her residency, Paige had learned to let go of matters beyond her control. Otherwise, every time you had to give bad news to a patient, it broke your heart. Not all women could succeed in bearing a child and not every illness could be cured. Now she brought that hard-earned focus to bear on her work. And the pregnant women of Safe Harbor cooperated by keeping her very, very busy.

Paige was on her feet all night with only a few breaks to catch a nap. She handled four uncomplicated deliveries, a breech birth in which she managed to get the baby safely turned around, and a Cesarean section that ushered a twin boy and girl into the world. Although they were a month early, they emerged alert and breathing on their own.

During a slow moment, Paige went to the nursery to

check on them. She found neonatologist Jared Sellers just finishing his examination of the boy.

"They both look great." The dark-haired young doctor rediapered the five-pound newborn. "Maybe they'll bring us good luck." His voice thickened with emotion.

"Of course they will!" she answered.

Jared's wife, Lori, Dr. Rayburn's nurse, had been trying for the past six months to get pregnant. About sixty percent of women became pregnant within that length of time, and although another fifteen percent achieved pregnancy naturally in the next three months, Lori was in her midthirties and worried about declining fertility. Last month, she'd come to see Paige and they'd begun checking her ovulation and hormone levels, along with Jared's sperm. So far, everything seemed fine, but further tests remained. The two of them joked about the fact that, since Lori had assisted at Paige's inseminations, they were helping each other get pregnant.

For a moment, Paige wondered if Jared was about to make a reference to her own situation, but he gave no sign that it even occurred to him. Good. Lori shouldn't have mentioned it, although Paige could imagine how easily confidential information might slip out when husband and wife worked at the same facility.

Instead, his entire attention riveted on the baby boy he was wrapping in a blanket. Tenderness and longing shone in his dark eyes.

How fortunate Lori was, to share her hopes and dreams with this loving husband. To have his encouragement through her monthly disappointments and, someday, his support during a pregnancy. Afterward, too, for all the years of child rearing.

A knot formed in Paige's chest. *If only...*

Oh, for heaven's sake! She didn't need a man like

Jared, or like Nora's doting Lock, or like Mike. Especially not like Mike. Although he didn't seem so obnoxious since she'd read him the riot act, in her current state of exhaustion and possible hormone flux, she couldn't be objective.

Fortunately, the nursery drew Paige's thoughts to a more pleasant subject. She moved about the dimly lit room peeking at the other infants she'd delivered tonight. All healthy, all contented in their bassinets. What adorable little people, with their wrinkly faces and tiny hands.

What would they look like in a few months, and in later years? She always loved when patients brought in their growing babies to show how they were developing. While she'd only practiced at Safe Harbor for eight months, she'd been with her previous group long enough to watch some of her patients' babies grow into the toddler years.

"I hope Lori gets pregnant soon," Paige said. "For your sake and, hey, I'll get credit in the contest."

Jared grinned. "I think it's totally unfair that only obstetricians get to participate."

"In consultation with our staff," Paige reminded him.

"The pediatricians and neonatologists get left out," he grumbled playfully. "Except for Samantha, of course."

In March, Dr. Tartikoff had announced a nine-month-long contest to spur staff morale, gain publicity and encourage use of the latest fertility techniques and procedures. The doctor who achieved the highest pregnancy rate among fertility patients would win a hundred-thousand-dollar donation to his or her favorite charity. Because the hospital didn't want to encourage potentially risky multiple births, each pregnancy counted only once, regardless of the number of babies per mom.

With such a large amount at stake, doctors had begun lobbying among their colleagues for their favorite causes.

Informal alliances had sprung up, with multiple doctors pledging to support the same charities. Pediatrician Samantha Forrest argued strongly for a community clinic she'd founded a few years ago to provide counseling and referrals to low-income families, women and teen mothers. Its chief competition came from a grant program proposed by obstetrician Zack Sargent to aid fertility patients who lacked insurance coverage for their treatments.

"I doubt I'll be anywhere near the front-runners," Paige observed. "I prefer to let patients proceed at their own pace rather than pushing them into in vitro."

"We appreciate that," Jared said. "There are some impressive new developments, but there's a price to be paid. Financially and physically."

"Not to mention emotionally," Paige pointed out.

"That, too."

She and Nora had an ongoing disagreement with Dr. T, who pressed for aggressive treatment of almost all cases. In Paige's opinion that did many patients a disservice, costing them thousands of dollars and putting them through procedures that might be unnecessary. On the other hand, it did increase their chances of conceiving quickly.

"Have you taken sides on the charity issue?" Jared asked as they walked out of the nursery.

"I guess I favor Zack's program. It would help some of my patients," Paige said. "The counseling center does fill a need, though. I'm especially concerned about the teen mothers."

"In my present mood, I'd vote for helping fertility patients," Jared remarked. "But I'm biased."

"Understandable."

In the hall, they went their separate ways. With a jolt, Paige saw that the small third-floor pharmacy was open. Overnight, only the larger second-floor pharmacy was staffed to meet urgent hospital demand. Now she had to deal with an issue she'd been postponing.

An overhead clock gave the time as 6:10 a.m. No wonder her eyes felt scratchy and she kept stifling yawns. She'd barely grabbed a couple of hours' sleep in the on-call room. *Not as young as I used to be.*

Paige's throat clenched. Why was she so reluctant to take a pregnancy test? Because it might come up negative—or because it might not?

When she'd left the labor and delivery ward, there'd been several women in labor. Any minute, she was likely to get beeped. And experience taught that babies conspired to come in a rush.

Better get this over with.

Gathering her courage, Paige went to pick up a pregnancy test kit.

THIS WAS MIKE'S IDEA of heaven. A plate of frozen waffles drenched in syrup—the good stuff, with real sugar—eaten with an appetite sharpened by the sea breeze. Lounging at the round patio table, he surveyed the cozy cottages across the street, their flower boxes cheery in the sunshine. The murmur of the surf and the mewing of seagulls were the only sounds to break the Sunday morning quiet.

At the neighbor's house, the front door slammed. A bleary-eyed woman in her twenties hauled a couple of suitcases toward a van in the driveway. Two more young women followed, loaded with skateboards, swim fins and scooters.

They were getting an early start, considering that their music hadn't cut off until nearly 2 a.m. Since the van bore Nevada plates, Mike figured they had a long drive ahead.

Under other circumstances, he'd have volunteered to

help them haul stuff. But in light of how inconsiderate they'd been, he decided to let the renters wrestle with their own luggage. Having found a parking space on the street last night, he had a clear view across the driveway as the less-than-ladies tried to stuff their gear into the van, snapping at each other all the while.

Life had a way of meting out fit punishments, he mused. Hangovers, for instance. He'd suffered his share of those in his younger days.

The breeze picked up, a pleasant counterpoint to the sunshine. Past the end of the street, the surf rumbled, and every now and then Mike caught the enthusiastic calls of surfers enjoying the higher-than-normal waves, the gift of a tropical storm off Mexico.

Despite the likelihood of more party animals to come, he'd sure relish living here. Dropping by his house yesterday to change clothes and grab his sleeping bag had reaffirmed how much he wanted to be gone before the newlyweds returned from their honeymoon. Paige's cottage might be small, but it was free of baby gear, it lay an easy stroll to the beach and it came with an Irish goddess in residence. Okay, not a goddess—a complicated woman.

That reminded him uneasily of something he'd noticed while fixing the bathroom door. Her magazine rack displayed a couple of medical journals, a women's magazine stuffed with diet and cooking tips, and a copy of *Today's Baby*.

Why would an obstetrician need a consumer-oriented baby magazine? Especially since he'd spotted her address printed on the cover. She hadn't subscribed out of idle curiosity.

He might be drawn to her like iron to a magnet. But long-term, this relationship didn't stand a chance. She was obviously the mom type, while his interest in babies ended with his nieces and nephews.

Mike stretched and listened to the murmur of the ocean. If only they could explore their mutual temptation without leaving either of them in emotional shreds.

The sight of an unshaven man shambling toward the van from the inland side yanked Mike from his musings. The women had gone indoors, leaving the vehicle wide-open, and the guy halted to assess its contents. His sunken cheeks and etched facial lines hinted of substance abuse, reminding Mike about the halfway house.

The man peered furtively around and shifted closer to the van. He didn't seem to notice Mike, probably due to the angle of the sun.

Sunlight flashed off a blue car turning from Seaside Lane. Mike's pulse tipped upward at the prospect of seeing Paige. Good thing he was here, in view of the uninvited visitor next door.

The garage door rolled up and she pulled straight in. The shaggy fellow remained by the van, watching. Purse over her shoulder, Paige strode out.

The man let out a wolf whistle that made her flinch. "Hey, babe. You're a long cool drink of water," he called. "Wanna get some breakfast?"

Paige shot him an irritated glance and clicked the garage door shut. "No, thanks."

The man edged onto the driveway, only a few yards from her. "It was a friendly offer. There's no need to be rude."

Mike had had enough. With deliberate slowness, he rose and straightened to his full height. "The lady said no."

The interloper cast one glance at Mike and shrugged. "Can't blame a guy for trying."

"Let me give you a tip. Women don't like being treated like sex objects." As he strolled toward them, Mike caught an appreciative twitch of Paige's mouth as he more or less quoted her own words.

"I wasn't…"

Paige joined in. "Don't call me babe. Don't tell me I'm a long drink of water. And when I frown at you, take a hint and leave me alone."

"Touchy, touchy."

Just then, one of the renters trudged out of the house carrying a large picnic basket and a stack of oversize towels. "Don't leave your van unguarded," Mike advised her. "This isn't a secure area."

"I didn't take anything!" protested Mr. Shaggy, a bit too quickly.

"Nobody said you did." Mike met the man's stare directly.

The guy's jaw wagged, but apparently he thought better of mouthing off. Bullies tended to back down when faced with an obviously superior force. That didn't, unfortunately, mean they'd been defanged.

As the creep turned and headed down the block, Paige shot Mike a grateful glance. "Thanks. I could have dealt with him but you made it a lot easier. Now if you'll excuse me, I'm beat." With a sleepy blink, she headed into the house.

"Yeah. Thanks from me, too." The woman next door pushed a lock of blonde hair from her cheek. "I haven't seen you around before."

"Lucky for you I was here this morning or you'd be minus some of your belongings." Mike didn't return her flirtatious tone. "You should exercise more caution."

"You sound like a cop," she grumbled.

"That's because I used to be one." Without waiting for

a reply, Mike followed Paige inside. He'd done the renter a favor by issuing a warning. If she and her buddies chose to learn their lessons the hard way, that was their right.

Finding Paige in the living room he said, "Sounds like you had a long night."

She nodded wearily. Even her once-crisp brown slacks and beige blouse seemed to droop. While he could see she must have worked hard, Mike got the sense something more was weighing on her.

He'd felt that way sometimes after a difficult shift, cleaning up the aftermath of a crime. No matter how hard he tried to toughen up, he couldn't shrug off everything. In the case of an obstetrician, he could imagine all sorts of things that might go wrong, and she was the kind of doctor who cared.

"Can I fix you waffles?" Mike offered. "They're whole wheat. I brought them from home."

For a moment, he thought she might decline. Then, as if releasing a burden, she said, "You know what? I'd like that very much."

They went into the kitchen. "Make yourself at home," he teased, indicating the round glass table near the front window. "There's coffee, too. Or will that keep you awake?"

"Not usually but I think I'll have herb tea," she said.

"I'll fix it." A kettle sat right on the stove, and Mike found the teabags in the adjacent cupboard.

She collapsed into a high-backed white chair. "I may never move again."

"You may not have to," he responded, and set to work with enthusiasm. Because in the past few minutes, an idea had taken shape.

Whatever was bothering Paige, she shouldn't have to cope with it alone. Mike just needed to get her in the right mood and he could solve both of their problems.

Chapter Six

Paige didn't want Mike Aaron to be the first person she told that she was pregnant. Yet the urge to confide in him was almost irresistible.

What a relief it had been when he confronted that jerk and sent him on his way. Also, after last night's break-in, she appreciated not having to worry about returning home alone. With his presence out front, Mike had been almost literally keeping watch on the house.

Now he was fixing her breakfast. When was the last time anyone had done that? Aunt Bree, before she got sick, but that had been years ago. And Bree hadn't had a powerful set of shoulders, lean hard hips and a teasingly masculine day's growth of beard.

I must be giddy from lack of sleep. Paige let her eyelids drift shut and inhaled the scent of waffles browning in the toaster oven. It eased the churning in her stomach.

"Falling asleep?" Mike's deep voice rumbled into her awareness.

"Close to it."

"Don't let me stop you."

She pried her eyelids open. "I'd better eat. I'll sleep more deeply and longer if I do."

"You don't have a problem sleeping during daylight?" he asked. "I had a hell of a time when I worked rotating shifts. Threw my whole body rhythm out of whack. I guess there's a medical term for that."

"Circadian rhythms," Paige replied, shifting instinctively into scientist mode. "People, animals, plants, even microbes are genetically programmed to follow roughly a 24-hour cycle, although we're also influenced by external cues such as light. There's a science that studies circadian rhythms, called chronobiology. *Chrono* comes from the Greek word for time."

"Wow." Mike slanted her an admiring grin. "No need to browse the internet with you around."

"We pack our brains with an immense amount in medical school. Unfortunately, that doesn't make doctors impervious to human weakness." Paige felt as if she'd used up her last ounce of energy with that recitation. She was glad when the kettle whistled, and Mike lifted it off the burner. He'd scrounged up a cup and teabag, she noticed. "You're handy in the kitchen."

"My parents ran a tight ship, with so many foster kids to take care of," he responded as he poured the steaming water. "We learned to cook, clean and do laundry. By the time I turned twelve, they made me third in command."

"Your sister's younger?"

"By three years." He set the cup and a spoon in front of her. "Sugar?"

"I take it plain. Smells wonderful." She let the fragrance waft over her. "So you were the big brother. Whereas I'm the kid sister, with five siblings who all believed they were the boss of me."

"You had to choose between fight and flight?"

"Ultimately, I chose both."

"Good for you." He set out a plate of waffles along with maple syrup, the real kind that Paige hadn't tasted in years. That further demonstrated his domestic value.

Domestic? There was a term she'd never expected to apply to Mike Aaron.

"Aren't you having any?" she asked.

"I already ate."

"Mind sitting with me?"

"Glad to."

When he took a seat opposite her, Paige released a long breath. While she didn't feel like confiding in Mike, she wasn't ready to be alone with her thoughts, either.

Since the moment when the stick turned blue, she'd been assailed by emotions from joy to anxiety. Yet she'd had no time to assimilate her reactions, with two more deliveries this morning.

One had gone smoothly. In the other birth, Paige had immediately recognized the indications of Down syndrome in the little girl: floppy muscle tone, a slightly flattened face with an upward slant to the eyes that didn't mirror the parents' appearance, plus a telltale single crease across the palms of the hands. Although the mother's physician had screened her, the test had failed to detect the disorder. While the diagnosis couldn't be confirmed without a chromosome study, Jared had recognized the signs also when Paige called him in. Thank goodness the neonatologist had still been at the hospital.

A short time later, she'd informed the stunned parents. She'd stayed with them after her twelve-hour shift until family members arrived along with their minister, who had a son with Down syndrome. While this couple faced a difficult road ahead, they had strong support. Paige hoped that, like another patient of hers, they'd find the child's learning and health issues more than counterbalanced by her overwhelming gift for love.

Paige knew better than to dwell on the possibility of something going wrong with her own child; a doctor could drive herself crazy that way. But the situation had arisen at a stressful time, just as she was trying to absorb the reality of her pregnancy. And it had taxed the last of her energy.

"I don't know what's going on with you, but I've come home from some night shifts so drained I could barely move," Mike commented gently.

Paige finished a mouthful of syrupy waffle. "It *was* a rough night. I don't usually fall apart like this."

"You aren't falling apart. No weeping, wailing or gnashing of teeth," he corrected. "And while my timing may not be ideal, I'd like to run something by you."

She knew instinctively he wanted to talk about moving in. How could she muster the strength to resist this kind, strong man who'd stood up for her when she needed him? But common sense warned that she must. "Mike…"

"Please hear me out." In the pure morning light, his gray eyes regarded her earnestly.

It was simpler to listen than to argue. Plus, she felt an inexplicable longing to delay the moment when she had to send him away. "Fine."

"I love the location. Also, I promised my brother I'd move out of my old place as soon as possible. Why not rent me the spare room for the summer?" As Mike spoke logically, Paige felt her resistance melting. "I can have my fun in the sun, and it'll give me a couple of months to find another place before fall."

Her better judgment warned her to grab an excuse, any excuse, to say no. Being around this man meant risking a relationship sure to end in disappointment. "Then I'll have to go through the whole housemate hunt again."

"Yes, but it will be easier in the fall," Mike continued. "I presume the house next door leases to someone steadier during the winter months." That was the usual pattern with beach rentals. "You'll have a quieter environment, which will make this place more attractive to a roommate."

"Good point." A pair of middle-aged male teachers had a standing arrangement to lease the place September through May. During the summers, when the rent quadrupled, they traveled. Last winter, after the halfway house opened, they'd served as a kind of buffer, which had made the past week since they moved out doubly unpleasant.

"You'll consider it?" Mike's jaw tightened as if biting down on further arguments.

Paige did some quick calculations. His proposal made a lot of sense. With her baby due in early February, she couldn't expect a roommate to stay past the first of the year anyway. If he moved out in September, she could decorate the nursery at her leisure, and—despite the excuse she made earlier—she wouldn't inconvenience some innocent roommate who expected to stay indefinitely.

That left one problem. A big one. Around him, her pregnancy-heightened senses quivered at the infusion of masculinity into the atmosphere. They'd be sharing a bathroom, lounging in the living room in bathrobes...and the mere prospect of seeing Mike in a swimsuit made her breasts tighten.

How could she put this delicately? "You and I don't exactly have a platonic relationship," Paige murmured. "Living together is asking for trouble."

With a twinkle, Mike said, "Did I mention that I called a glass-repair service last night? There's a repairman coming to fix your door at three o'clock."

One more matter she didn't have to worry about. Paige wasn't sure whether to laugh or cry. "That's cheating."

"Just my way of showing how useful I can be." Mike quirked an eyebrow as if encouraging her to say yes.

"Doesn't change the situation." She wished she sounded more decisive. Paige hadn't felt this vulnerable since her teen years, when she fought off her family's opposition to her majoring in premed at the University of Texas. Then, she'd relied on Aunt Bree's support, through letters and phone calls, to bolster her confidence. Now, she had no one to lean on.

No one but Mike. And the longer he sat here regarding her hopefully, the more powerful her inclination to yield.

He indicated her empty plate. "Want more?"

Yes, but she'd better not. "Thanks, but no." *And that goes for your suggestion about moving in, too.* Yet somehow the words failed to reach her mouth.

Mike stretched. His legs bumped hers, and it took a moment to shift around and arrange themselves so both pairs of extra-long limbs had room. "Sorry about that." He didn't sound sorry, though.

Paige struggled to make her point. "Mike, let's get back to the asking-for-trouble part."

"If you don't want it to happen, it won't," he countered coolly.

"That's the problem," she admitted.

"Why does it have to be a problem?"

"Because while we might have a good time, I don't believe we're compatible in the long run." She hoped he wasn't going to get his feelings hurt, because this had nothing to do with him. *If I weren't pregnant...* But she was.

"Neither do I," he said calmly.

Ouch. "Oh?"

"I'm open to whatever happens between us." He gave a small shrug. "Maybe nothing. Maybe a lot of fun. Likely things won't work out in the long-term. If that bothers you, I promise to keep my hands and other body parts to myself. The last thing I want is a messy situation."

She felt an unexpected pang of disappointment. "Even though I agree with you, I'm curious why you're so sure we're incompatible."

"I saw the baby magazine in the bathroom."

Paige caught her breath. "So?" Surely he didn't guess that she was pregnant. Even a detective couldn't be that sharp.

"You want kids." Mike shook his head.

"And you don't?"

He folded his hands on the table. "Growing up, I got my fill of mentoring kids and living in chaos. I'm strictly an adults-only kind of guy. When I was younger, people told me I'd change my mind. Well, I'm thirty-three. That's old enough to be sure."

She shouldn't feel so let down, Paige chided herself. Even if he didn't have an aversion to babies, she could hardly expect him to raise another man's child.

Oddly, the certainty that they had no future together proved reassuring. She needn't worry about false expectations on either of their parts. And right now she felt a lot safer with a man in the house, especially one as capable as Mike. Why not keep him around for the summer?

"I love the way your thoughts show on your face," Mike said. "It's better than an action movie."

"Watch the teasing. You might make me reconsider," she warned.

An off-center grin lit his face. "Does that mean I'm in?"

"We'll need ground rules," Paige warned. "About privacy, neatness, inviting friends over and so on."

"I'm housebroken, I assure you." Mike sat back, clearly

pleased. "And I happen to like rules. They let everyone know where they stand."

When he smiled that way, Paige had to fight the impulse to cup his handsome, scratchy face with her palm. "I'll prorate the rent since we're already a week into the month."

"Don't worry about it." He piled her empty cup atop her plate. "Also, since I'll be borrowing a truck, I can move out your old furniture if you'll tell me where to take it."

She'd seen a notice on the bulletin board that morning seeking donations for a fundraising yard sale sponsored by Samantha Forrest's counseling center. "Can I give you that address tomorrow? You're welcome to use the bed or the couch till then."

"Works for me." Mike carried the dishes to the sink.

As she arose stiffly, Paige hoped she'd made the right decision. Because one way or the other, life around here was about to change.

Chapter Seven

On the drive to work Monday morning, Mike monitored a local news and traffic radio service that worked with the police department. It didn't entirely substitute for a police scanner, but law enforcement communications were encrypted these days. Fortunately, the Safe Harbor police chief liked to get the news out to the public in the belief that transparency boosted trust.

Nothing major seemed to be going on today: a traffic collision on Safe Harbor Boulevard, with a recommendation to use alternate routes; illegal fireworks confiscated from a home, and a warning about the dangers they presented. On the human-interest side, the announcer explained that the fire department had declined to mount a rescue for a cat stuck in a tree. To any outraged animal lovers in the audience, he asked when they'd last seen a cat skeleton in a tree. The answer was undoubtedly "never," since felines had a talent for scrambling down on their own.

Mike hummed happily. He'd had a productive Sunday—made sure the glass in Paige's back door got fixed properly and the alarm reattached, arranged to borrow a pickup from a pal at the police department, and figured out where in the living room to place his big-screen TV. Incredibly, all Paige owned was a tiny set in her bedroom. How could anyone live like that?

Last night at his old house, despite being surrounded by his possessions, he'd felt as if he were just visiting. Already, the beach cottage had become home.

Mike turned onto Lyons Way and into the parking lot of a strip mall dominated by the Sexy Over Sixty gym and Lyons Way Escrow. Most people arriving here wouldn't even notice the door between them lettered Fact Hunter Investigations, with the offices located on the second floor. Being discreet suited the agency's clients, those few who chose to come here in person.

A little over a year ago, Mike and Lock had bought the agency from a former marine and retired cop named Bruce Hunter. Despite the ongoing challenge of bringing in enough revenue to cover expenses, pay employees and earn a modest profit, Mike liked being his own boss. While earning a master's degree in criminal science, Mike had spent three years with the Orange County Sheriff's Department, then eight at the Safe Harbor P.D. That was enough of following other people's orders.

While some guys figured he was crazy to give up a steady paycheck and a pension, Mike had ambitions. In another half-dozen years, he might run for the powerful job of county sheriff. He considered it a plus to have the experience of owning a firm and making connections in the business world.

He parked to the side, leaving spaces open for customers, although most often he met clients at their homes or offices, or dealt with them by phone or email. His steadiest sources of income were contracts with a couple of local companies including Kendall Technologies, but he also drew clients from the internet, the Yellow Pages and referrals.

The display on his watch said 7:47. Although the agency didn't open until nine, he preferred to arrive early, especially this week, when they were shorthanded.

His laptop case slung over one shoulder, Mike unlocked the outer door and collected the fliers and envelopes that had dropped through the mail slot on Saturday. Usually, he worked that morning, but Erica had asked him to chauffeur some out-of-town wedding guests. All safely returned home by now or enjoying West Coast vacations.

Inside, a steep staircase led to the second floor. To his right, a small sign pointed the way to the service elevator. Not an ideal setup but handicapped clients usually preferred to have an agent come to them, anyway.

Mike took the stairs at a fast clip, unlocked a second door and stepped into his domain. Pristine paint and carpeting, along with framed certificates and commendations, emphasized the office's professionalism. A few chairs and couches—although he rarely kept anyone waiting—faced the reception desk that in another hour would be staffed by Sue Carrera, the bilingual secretary who'd worked for the previous owner. Mike also spoke fluent Spanish, which had proved useful with foster kids and in his police work.

The suite held private offices for Lock and Mike, plus a report-writing room that doubled as an archive and as Patty's base of operations. Mike was glad she'd decided to leave the police department and work for him, a decision that was paying off now that she'd married and had a six-year-old stepdaughter. Although she put in some odd hours and occasional weekends, she had a lot of scheduling flexibility.

Mike was also glad he didn't have to deal with the time

conflicts that went along with child rearing. In his opinion, that really held a person back on the job.

As he switched on his laptop, he glanced around the office to make sure it looked presentable for a client. On Friday, as usual, he'd cleared the broad desk. Aside from a file cabinet and framed certifications on the walls, the place made no pretense at decor. Not likely to impress Mrs. Jones, but a cut above the messy P.I. offices in the movies.

After opening a window—air-conditioning just didn't keep the place fresh enough to suit Mike—he sorted through the mail, discarding the junk and tucking the bills into a drawer. Then he took out his reading glasses and sat down to read his email.

At 8:45, he heard Sue arrive and soon afterward he smelled coffee. A few minutes later, Patty stuck her head in the door. Short, straight blonde hair topped her square face as she called out her standard, "Hey, boss."

"How's it going?" he asked.

"Just ducky." She beamed. The down-to-earth detective had been blooming with happiness since last November, when she'd married Alec Denny, the hospital's embryologist. "Heard anything from Lock?"

"I hope he has better things to do on his honeymoon than call his brother."

"Gotcha. Hey, you and the doctor cut quite a figure on the dance floor." She eyed him curiously. "I thought you two didn't hit it off." She'd witnessed their first meeting a year ago, when his remark about Amazons had annoyed Paige.

Although Mike didn't like discussing private matters, his change of address would soon be public knowledge. "I'm renting a room from her for the summer. She has a place at the beach."

Patty's eyebrows shot up. "You're living with her?"

"That would be correct." Mike nearly added that it was a platonic arrangement, but why bother? It was none of her business and, besides, he didn't plan for it to stay platonic.

"What's this?" On tiptoe, Sue Carrera peered over Patty's shoulder. "You're moving in with someone?" A child-free divorcée in her midfifties, the secretary adored any whiff of romance among her fellow staffers.

"I'm renting a room," Mike corrected.

"You did mention you were looking for a house." Sue sounded disappointed.

"Found one. I'll email you the new address." Enough of this subject. "I've got a new client coming at ten. Name she gave was Mrs. Jones."

"I'll set up a file." Sue departed, as did Patty. Neither looked entirely satisfied.

A short while later, Mike was reviewing his and Patty's schedules for the week when he heard Sue call out, "Hi. Can I help you?"

"Mrs. Jones, to see Detective Aaron." The impatient female voice sounded vaguely familiar.

It was 9:55. Very punctual, he thought, and closed the file.

"If you'll just sign in—"

"I prefer not to sign anything. Just let him know I'm here."

Where had he heard that patrician tone with its strident edge? Mike did his best to remember everyone he met, particularly those in business and local government.

Even though the woman had given an alias, her manner implied she expected red-carpet treatment. And if she was who he suspected, no wonder.

Springing to his feet, Mike went to greet the mayor's wife.

EVEN THOUGH SHE'D SHEPHERDED hundreds of women over the course of nine months and helped bring their babies into the world, by Monday morning Paige still hadn't fully grasped the reality of being pregnant. So many things to consider, so many plans to make. And, at the moment, so many hormones to contend with.

Launching her body into action had never been difficult before. Today, she longed to pull the covers over her head; then, to linger in the shower. At breakfast, she missed having Mike pamper her, although cereal and milk with a side of orange juice was healthier than waffles.

She also missed her usual coffee, since the brew tasted impossibly bitter. But she *did* enjoy the soothing rumble of the surf and the delightful childish laughter from next door, where a young couple with two children had replaced the party girls.

Her peaceful, settled mood didn't last long. Arriving at the medical building, Paige was hit by the obnoxious odor of disinfectant suffusing the elevator. She supposed the cleaning crew used it regularly, but she'd barely noticed it before. Well, she should get in the habit of climbing the stairs to the second floor, anyway.

After greeting the receptionist and nurse, she hurried into her office to check her email before the first patient arrived. In the queue, a staff message from Dr. T leaped out. He reported that the pregnancy rate for the first three months of the contest failed to meet his expectations. In fact, he noted sternly, he himself had achieved the highest rate, and the rest of them had better step it up. Translation: Push your patients into more aggressive treatment.

Although Dr. T was bound to be crankier than usual with his favorite scrub nurse gone for the week, Paige didn't appreciate the pressure. Still, as a new staff member, she was hardly in a position to complain.

She deleted the message, along with the usual newsletters and other routine items, and responded to inquiries from patients. Concerned about the woman who'd delivered the baby with Down syndrome, Paige was glad to see a message from the patient's regular physician. He thanked her for the extra care and promised to follow up with whatever referrals the couple needed.

With the emails out of the way, Paige noted that this morning's schedule was jam-packed with physicals, surgical follow-ups, maternity care and fertility cases. From the outer office, she heard voices. The day had truly begun.

By 10 a.m., a caffeine headache reminded her of those missing cups of coffee. As Paige fixed a stronger-than-usual cup of tea in the break room, she listened to the nasal drone of her nurse, Keely Randolph, confirming a patient's list of medications. Like Paige, Keely was substituting for a staffer on leave—in this case, Dr. T's wife, Bailey, who was Nora's regular nurse.

Paige resisted the temptation to sit down. If she did, she might close her eyes and yield to those hormones whispering subversive nonsense about taking a nap.

While sipping the tea, she reviewed the next patient's chart on a computer screen. Sheila Obermeier was a healthy thirty-two-year-old who'd been seeing Nora for regular checkups. Last month, she'd come to Paige for help in getting pregnant, after a fruitless year of trying on her own. She had no obvious medical issues or medications that might interfere, and in the past few weeks they'd begun the basic fertility workup. Some test results had come back on Friday.

"Patient's prepped." Keely's large frame filled the entrance. As usual, she wore a stubborn expression.

Working with Keely was, to Paige, like pushing an overloaded shopping cart with a skewed wheel. What a frustrating waste of energy. Still, in the end, you got your groceries to the checkout line just the same.

"Thank you." She cleared away her cup.

With a grunt, the nurse disappeared, probably to vent her ill temper on the young receptionist. Paige felt sorry for the girl, but hesitated to intervene unless Keely did something completely out of line. Although the doctors at Safe Harbor maintained private practices, most contracted with the hospital for staffing. Until Bailey or Nora returned, Paige was stuck with the disagreeable woman.

In the hallway, she knocked and then entered the patient's room. On the examining table sat a tense fair-haired woman in a hospital gown. "Did you find anything?"

"Good news. Your tests came back normal," Paige assured her, and proceeded to explain the results. She concluded, "Our next step is to make sure the sperm isn't the problem. I see your husband hasn't provided a specimen."

"He keeps putting it off. He says he's busy at work."

"I was hoping he'd accompany you on this visit." Paige had suggested that the last time she saw the woman.

Sheila rolled her eyes. "You don't know Gil!"

True enough. "It's important that we discuss his concerns." Some men took the possibility of a sperm deficit as a challenge to their masculinity.

"He keeps saying I'm young and there's no hurry. I left my first husband because he didn't want children. That's why I took up with Gil in the first place, and now he's pulling the same routine, only he isn't as honest about it." A sheen in her eyes warned of tears.

Paige had learned that an unruffled attitude was helpful to patients, so she continued smoothly, "Do you believe your husband doesn't want kids? Surely he's aware that you stopped using birth control."

"Yes, not that I gave him much choice. He *said* he wanted them. But now…" The words ended in a sniffle.

"He's changed his mind?"

"Or something. I sure hope I didn't dump my first husband for more of the same. Sometimes I wish I'd given Mike more time. Looking back, I guess I was trying to punish him by hooking up with Gil, and then things spun out of control."

Mike? Paige scrolled down the computer screen. There it was. Sheila Aaron Obermeier. She hadn't made the connection before. No reason why she should have, of course.

Paige would never discuss a patient with anyone other than a medical supervisor, but what about the reverse situation? In a small town like Safe Harbor, especially given the likelihood of continuing contact between ex-spouses, full disclosure seemed the best course.

As Paige weighed her words, she noticed how pretty Sheila was, petite with large eyes and a full mouth. *Not an Amazon like me.* Annoyed at the unprofessional thought, she said, "I didn't realize I knew your ex-husband. Coincidentally, he just rented a room from me for the summer."

"For the summer?" her patient asked, puzzled.

"I have a place near the beach and I advertised for a roommate," Paige explained. "If that's a problem, I can arrange for you to see another doctor until Dr. Franco returns. It shouldn't disrupt your care."

Sheila shrugged. "No big deal. I feel comfortable with you, and anyway, most of the ob-gyns around here are men. I prefer a woman. It's like you're on my side."

"I hope we're all on the same side." If the husband wasn't on board with having a child, that indicated major problems beyond the scope of a medical office. Still, a doctor treated the whole patient, and to some extent that included the state of her marriage. "I'd like to meet Gil.

Do you think he'd talk to me on the phone? I might be able to persuade him to come in."

"Quite the opposite. I'm sure he'd convince you of whatever he wants you to believe." Sheila made a face. "He's an insurance salesman. Smooth talker. I thought he loved me and wanted a family, but now I'm not so sure." A tear slid down her cheek.

"Have you discussed your concerns?" To Paige, that seemed a no-brainer, but in her practice, she'd found that some spouses didn't communicate well.

"We just end up arguing." Sheila accepted the proffered box of tissues. "Thanks."

Paige leaned against the counter near the sink. "We can't proceed without his cooperation. It isn't fair to subject you to invasive procedures until we rule out a problem with the sperm."

Sheila blew her nose. "You're right. I mean, the least he can do is accompany me to a visit. Then the ball will be in your court, Dr. Brennan."

"I'll do my best." Finessing a reluctant husband into a sperm test wasn't one of the subjects covered in medical school. However, a meeting ought to give Paige a clearer perspective on the situation. "If he can't come in on a weekday, perhaps we could work in a consult at the hospital while I'm on call."

"One way or the other, I'll drag his tail in here," Sheila replied. "He owes it to me."

As they wrapped up the visit, Paige hoped the couple wasn't having serious problems. She'd seen the heartbreak when a woman became pregnant just as her marriage disintegrated. One of her patients, abandoned by a cheating husband, had become so distraught she let her sister adopt the baby.

A few minutes later, as Paige jotted her notes, Sheila's

words replayed through her mind. *I was trying to punish him by hooking up with Gil.* She couldn't imagine cheating on her husband just to get back at him.

Still, one thing was obvious: Mike had apparently sacrificed his marriage rather than become a father. If she'd harbored any delusions about a future together, that put them to rest.

Tamping down a twinge of frustration, she pulled up the chart for her next patient.

Chapter Eight

The last time Mike encountered Gemma Hightower had been a few months earlier at a chamber of commerce mixer. Her husband, Roy, who owned a real estate brokerage, had been doing double duty at the event. A long-time member of the city council, he'd been elevated to the part-time position of mayor this past January but still had to keep his company solvent in a tough market. So, while representing the city, he'd also been glad-handing potential clients.

His wife had circulated, head high, acknowledging people with a nod. She'd only paused to speak to those who'd earned their way into her social circle through charity work or connections.

Gemma Hightower, alias Mrs. Jones, still wore a regal air and quite a few thousand bucks' worth of designer clothing as she sat across the desk from Mike, but today anger flashed from her narrowed eyes. Despite the hard-set mouth, no lines disturbed the smoothness of her skin. In her midfifties, the town's first lady kept up her guard in the battle against aging.

"What makes you think your husband is cheating on you?" Mike asked.

An involuntary start shook her thin frame, but failed

to dislodge a single hair from the honey-colored chignon. "Why do you assume that?"

Experience. "If I'm wrong, please correct me."

He half expected her to swoop to her feet and stalk out. Instead, her shoulders sagged. "The Kendalls said you were trustworthy. And that you'd be discreet."

"Absolutely." He was glad one of his major clients spoke highly of him. Perhaps it had been Reese Kendall's young wife, Persia, who'd passed the word along. In her early twenties, the exotic former executive trainee at Kendall Technologies had quickly taken her place among the cream of Safe Harbor society. "How long has the affair been going on?"

The question seemed to startle her all over again. Most likely she'd expected to control the interview, but that wasn't how Mike handled things.

She recouped quickly. "Longer than most."

"Most?"

"I'm not naive, Detective. Roy and I have been married nearly thirty years. He's a good-looking man in a position of authority. Women gravitate to him." She seemed to take pride in that fact.

His wife must carry an image of him from thirty years ago, since the jowly Roy Hightower didn't fit Mike's idea of a handsome man. Yet if she was right, at least one other woman found him attractive. "He's had affairs before?"

"Nothing of substance." She swallowed. "When I smelled perfume, well, I didn't make too much of that. Then the phone calls started."

Mike scratched "phone calls" on a pad. While it would be more convenient to take notes in the computer, that tended to bother clients, particularly in a personal matter. "Tell me about them."

"A few months ago, the phone began to ring at odd hours. When I answer, there's no one there." She scowled.

"Does Roy ever pick them up?"

"If he answers the phone and starts talking to someone, how would I know if it's the mystery caller?" she snapped.

"I meant, has he ever mentioned hang-ups?" He adjusted his reading glasses. Not only did they help with the paperwork involved in running the agency, he'd also learned that they softened his appearance and made some clients more comfortable.

"No. But he's in a prominent position. Some council votes are controversial. I'm sure he'd take that sort of thing in stride."

He never mentioned them and you never asked. Not exactly a close relationship, Mike mused. "Did you notify the phone company?"

Her nostrils flared. "I don't wish to involve anyone official."

"Understood." His thoughts returned to the nature of the phone calls. While a mistress would have Roy's cell number, she might call the house if the in-box was full or the cell turned off. Or to disturb the wife, hoping to spark a confrontation and divorce. "Ever hear anyone breathing or whispering on the line?"

"No." Gemma folded her hands tightly. "But I did notice a pattern."

"What kind of pattern?"

"If I don't answer immediately, there are two rings and then it stops. Then one more ring and then it stops again."

That *was* strange. "Has he ever used coded signals like that with you?"

She stared at him coldly. "Why on earth would he? Anyway, I dismissed it as someone's idea of a prank. Then this past month, there were gifts."

"Someone's sending anonymous gifts?" That didn't fit the usual signs of an affair. Still, it might be another tactic to spark a fight and clear the path to become Wife Number Two.

"No. I meant, my husband began giving me gifts." The woman rattled a diamond-and-sapphire bracelet on her slim wrist. "Expensive ones."

"Did you ask him why?"

"He said I deserved them for putting up with the hard times." Her mouth twitched in suspicion.

"You think he's salving a guilty conscience?" Mike asked.

Gemma leaned forward, her high cheekbones dotted with angry red spots. "What bothers me is that he's probably giving the same jewelry to his mistress, and we can't afford it. With the real estate market so unpredictable, his business nearly went under. That's confidential."

"Everything you tell me is confidential," Mike confirmed, and made another note.

"This weekend, he was out of town at a conference. He got careless and left his list of passwords in an unlocked desk drawer." Her mouth curved in a bitterly triumphant smile.

"Any interesting emails?"

"He'd deleted them all." She folded her arms. "Then I went into his credit card account online."

Good move. "Did you print out what you found?"

From her designer purse, Gemma pulled a sheaf of papers. "Here."

Mike scanned the charges. The name of a jewelry store jumped out, with three purchases in the ten thousand dollar range. "Are these all items you received?"

"Yes." For having received such generous gifts, she showed no signs of pleasure.

"Does he have any other credit cards?"

"Two. One business, one personal. I checked them both," she said. "He pays his bills online and his bank didn't list any other cards."

"Any hotels or motels?"

"No, but he did charge a lot of meals at an expensive Continental restaurant in Orange, where he's less likely to be recognized. Those go back nearly a year. It's longer than he's ever fooled around with anyone until now."

Evidently she'd snooped on her husband before. "Did you print out a copy of his bank deposits and checks?"

"There were no checks that I consider suspicious. Other than that, I don't see that our financial situation is any of your business," she replied tautly. "In case you're wondering, I accessed his business accounts, as well. I didn't see any jewelry purchases or hotel bills. As for his credit card for city-related expenses, that gets audited. He isn't stupid."

While Roy might be hiding his purchases in any number of ways, the man was hardly a financial wizard. And he hadn't been terribly clever about the passwords. *Unless he deliberately left them for her to find, to allay her suspicions.* Mike decided to accept the situation, for now. "This doesn't necessarily add up to an affair," he told her. "He could be putting together a sensitive business deal."

"For an entire year?" She shook her head. "If he were, I'd have got wind of it by now."

Mike asked a few more questions. Since real estate brokers often worked evenings and weekends, his absences didn't prove anything, and Roy had always dressed well. He hadn't taken off his wedding ring, but then, if his mistress knew the home phone number, she realized he was married. No new musical interests or catch phrases that might indicate he was socializing with someone much younger.

Gemma blanched when Mike asked whether her husband had tried any new approaches to lovemaking. "That's revolting!"

"It's a common sign that someone's learning those things during an affair."

"I always considered that a plus," she said, and flushed bright red. Quickly, she added, "Nothing out of the ordinary, thank heaven."

This might not be Mike's idea of a good marriage, but he wasn't here to judge. "Our next step is to try to spot him with this woman. Discreetly, of course."

"Once he gets his business back on solid ground, he's planning to run for the state assembly." She shot Mike a that's-confidential glance. "I've stood by him all these years. I'm not giving up my position to be one of those pathetic cast-off wives that nobody invites anywhere. Also, it would devastate our son. Gary's away at college, but he still depends on us emotionally and financially."

Although Mike suspected a guy that age would handle his parents' divorce well enough, she was entitled to her opinion. "Since Mr. Hightower might recognize me, I'll assign one of my other agents to keep an eye on him."

Her hand shot up in a Stop! gesture. "I don't want anyone else involved. Can't you do this yourself?"

"It adds to the risk of getting spotted, but if you prefer..."

"I do."

"Please understand that to tail him would require several agents, and it would be hard to avoid notice in such a small town," Mike explained. "I'd rather try to pinpoint the days and times when he's most likely to meet this woman, and try to spot him at the restaurant. My guess is that she might live near there. If they're meeting at her place, that would explain the absence of motel bills."

"That did occur to me."

He couldn't resist asking one more question. "Why so concerned about this affair, aside from the fact that it's lasted longer than most?"

Gemma blinked in what appeared to be irritation. "There are just…anomalies. If necessary, I'll persuade her to break it off without having to confront Roy. There are ways, believe me. Perfectly legal ways."

"I see." It sounded as if she'd done this before. She must have taken his previous affairs more seriously than she'd indicated.

They squared away the matter of Mike's retainer, which Mrs. Hightower paid from a bank account her husband didn't know about. She also provided a copy of the mayor's schedule for the next few weeks, as far as she knew it.

With a fluid motion, she rose. "Do you carry a gun, Mr. Aaron?"

"I have a carry permit," he said. While he wore a .38 on a belt and kept a smaller weapon strapped to his ankle in case someone managed to disarm him, she didn't need to know that.

"Well, don't shoot him until I figure out what I want to do."

"I'll try not to." Mike hoped he'd never have to shoot anyone. In his law-enforcement career, he'd drawn his gun many times but fired shots only twice. Once, a gunman had gone down in a hail of bullets from three officers, and the other time both Mike and his opponent had missed. He'd wrestled the guy to the ground and cuffed him.

When they shook hands, hers was cool and dry. Escorting her out of the office, Mike resolved to keep her file to himself.

He had no idea what kind of situation they were dealing with or who Roy might be boffing, if anyone. Political careers hung in the balance, and a misstep could hurt Mike's reputation as much as Roy's.

He had to be careful.

ON SUNDAY, PAIGE stood sipping a cup of tea and wondering what Aunt Bree would think of her living room now. The blue sofa and off-white armchairs faced a giant TV screen instead of each other, and she'd had to move the shadow boxes into her bedroom to make space. As for the grandfather clock in the corner, while she'd always found the soft chimes soothing, she'd stopped winding it after Mike spilled his beer when it went off while he was watching a game. It had never kept accurate time, anyway.

On Tuesday evening, he'd arrived with a pickup truck and a couple of muscular friends to cart off the extra furniture, which Dr. Forrest had been thrilled to receive for her center's yard sale. The guys had returned with far more belongings than Paige had expected. There'd been a slight problem finding a place for his treadmill, but Mike had measured the garage and found just enough room to wedge it into the back right corner, as long as she parked carefully. He'd managed to stow everything else neatly by last night, when his friends arrived to watch a DVD of motorcycle racing.

Paige wasn't accustomed to the rumble of high-powered motors or the soaring level of testosterone in her small house. However, the fact that these were police officers more than compensated. With them around, she didn't have to worry about intruders.

Mike's buddies had departed by eleven. From her bedroom, where she'd been catching up on medical journals, Paige had listened to the unfamiliar sounds of a man moving about her house. Even with her door closed, everything felt different. Smelled different. Echoed differently.

She heard water running in the bathroom and a tuneless hum as Mike washed up. How strange to know his razor was curled on the counter next to her hair dryer and his toothbrush angled beside hers in the holder. And that he was showering in the same tub where she stood naked every morning.

Paige had pulled the covers tighter around her and torn her thoughts away. She didn't want to picture Mike's muscular back and narrow waist, which she recalled in far too much detail from when she'd seen him at the beach.

To restore her concentration, she'd tossed the journals aside and thumbed through a baby magazine. That only substituted one temptation for another. Now Paige had to resist the urge to go on the internet and order a crib, a changing table, toys, picture books, a diaper stacker and all those other darling items featured in the ads. As she advised her patients, it was wise to wait until after the first trimester. In addition, she pointed out to them, friends and relatives were likely to give many of those items as gifts.

Gifts. Showers. Excited family members. How would her sisters react? And her brothers, for that matter? Although she didn't want to deal with them yet, she longed for someone to talk to.

This morning, Mike had gone out early for a jog. Besides, Paige wasn't about to discuss her pregnancy with *him*.

Suddenly she realized who she wanted to talk to. Crazy as it seemed, she needed to share her situation with Aunt

Bree. Relieved at the thought, Paige deposited her empty teacup to the kitchen and went to grab a jacket against the morning chill.

THE MORNING BREEZE WHIPPED away the heat as Mike jogged along the beach. Despite the cushioning effect of the sand, his muscles burned and his shoulders were beginning to ache. He'd run west nearly to the city limits and back again, but it wasn't far enough to escape his dilemma.

Spying on Roy Hightower had proved ridiculously easy, thanks to the guy's predictable habits. On Friday, Mike had spotted him entering the Continental restaurant Gemma had named, and a few minutes later he'd seen a woman go inside.

A woman Mike recognized. A woman he knew to be predatory, hard as nails and physically dangerous should Gemma confront her.

About an hour later, the pair had emerged together. He'd captured shots of Roy's arm around Yelena Yerchenko's waist and her hand slipping into his pants. They'd paused and shared a kiss, her ripe body pressing into his fleshy one. Not very subtle, in full public view in the middle of the day. Roy seemed too caught up in his lust for a blonde woman a decade his junior to think about consequences.

When they departed in separate cars, Mike had debated following them, but what more proof did he need of their affair? Anyway, he'd had to duck to avoid being seen as Yelena passed. No question that she would recognize him.

For one thing, she owned Lyons Way Escrow, right next door to Mike's office. For another, a couple of years ago when he worked at the police department, he'd investigated a nasty assault case in which she'd nearly gouged out her boyfriend's eye with a kitchen knife. The guy had contended it was an unprovoked attack motivated by jealousy; she'd pointed to a bruise on her cheek and claimed self-defense.

During the investigation, Mike had noted her lack of remorse despite the severe injury to the boyfriend and the way she turned her charm on and off as it suited her. He'd also picked up inconsistencies in her statements. In the end, the D.A. had considered it mutual combat and declined to file charges against either of the pair.

Now, while Mike had an obligation to report the facts to his client, the possibility that he might be throwing Gemma Hightower in the path of a violent sociopath disturbed him. Also, Yelena's involvement with the mayor struck him as odd. Unlike Roy, the boyfriend had been good-looking and younger than her. Nor was Roy wealthy enough to hold on to Yelena for an entire year, even if he was giving her jewelry that hadn't showed up on his credit cards.

That line of thinking brought him back to Gemma's possible danger. If Yelena had set her sights on marrying Roy and rising to prominence as the wife of a political up-and-comer, she wasn't likely to let his current wife stand in her way.

He'd caution Mrs. Hightower, of course. And with Yelena running a business right next door to Mike's, he'd need to subcontract out any further surveillance to avoid being recognized.

Ahead on the nearly empty beach, he saw a tall, slim figure gazing at the sand. A fiery cloud of hair billowed about her, setting the horizon ablaze. Why was he worrying about the Hightowers on this splendid morning, when the woman who'd teased him all night in his dreams stood gloriously before him?

As she bent to pluck something from the ground, Mike slowed his pace. No use trying to catch his breath, though. Paige Brennan had just stolen it all over again.

Chapter Nine

When Paige went to the beach to talk to her aunt, the way they'd often walked and exchanged confidences in the past, she'd hoped that expressing her uncertainties would calm her restlessness. The ocean stood in for a gravesite, since Aunt Bree had chosen to have her ashes scattered at sea, and it seemed only natural to come here to seek insight.

What Paige hadn't expected was an answer. Perhaps two.

There in the sand nestled a glimmer of rare purple sea glass. Among several hundred pieces of the ocean-buffed shards, Paige had found only one purple bit previously, a few years ago. As they exclaimed over it, Bree had told her with mock solemnity, "Now I know what to send you as a sign after I'm gone, the way people send pennies from heaven dated with their birth year."

"Don't be silly," Paige had told her. "I don't believe in that stuff."

Now here it was. And as she straightened, she saw the man who'd figured prominently in her silent confessions pacing toward her along the beach. An amber T-shirt clung damply to Mike's broad chest, while tan shorts displayed the toned power of his legs. The man might be utterly wrong for her, but his firm stride and curving mouth sent a delicious trembling through her knees.

Was this part of Bree's answer, or mere coincidence? Paige cleared her throat. "Good morning."

"What did you find?" As Mike halted alongside, his large hand cupped hers. Warmth burst around her while he examined the polished shape.

"Sea glass. It's a rare color, possibly from an old perfume bottle."

"You collect these." Of course, he'd seen the shadow boxes. "It glows like a precious gem. What're those purple stones called?"

"Amethysts." She wasn't sure why, but she added, "My Aunt Bree and I used to enjoying hunting for these. She always said if she wanted to send me a sign from the afterlife, it would be purple glass."

"A sign of what?"

That was hard to answer. "Reassurance. Approval. Maybe a nudge in the right direction, assuming I can figure out what that is." Quickly, to avoid mentioning the subject of her thoughts, she said, "What makes the glass special is that it has a history, even if I may never know the details. It might have fallen from a ship far away, or been carried off by an ancient wave."

"How romantic." The hard planes of his face softened as he gazed at her.

"In olden times, people believed that whenever a sailor died, mermaids would cry, and their tears turned into glass." Paige stopped. Why was she enthusing about this to Mike Aaron, of all people?

As he released her hand, his gaze slid down her denim jacket to her embroidered jeans. Irritated, she braced for a crack about how much he'd preferred her in a bikini.

Instead, his deep voice said, "Shall we walk? I guess I'm like you. I need to cool down in motion."

"Sure." Although it felt strange to be strolling together as if they were old friends, Paige set out alongside him.

"How did you get so interested in sea glass?" Mike asked as a teenage girl trotted past with two small dogs straining at their leashes.

"Originally, I planned to collect shells." Paige had quickly dropped that idea. "That was until I discovered that the little animals were sometimes still inside them. Even when they'd died, you have to boil the shells to preserve them."

"And keep them from smelling to high heaven?"

Her nose wrinkled. "You got that right."

They crossed a grassy area where a couple of children were playing Frisbee with their parents. Paige estimated their ages at around three and five, a tiny girl and a sturdy boy. Which would her baby be? She had names picked out already: Bree for a girl, Brian for a boy.

Mike's voice penetrated her thoughts. "Is there a way to figure out where the glass comes from?"

"Sometimes you can tell by the color." Paige had researched the subject on the internet. "Certain shades come from plates that used to be given away as prizes during the Depression era. Others come from whiskey and soda bottles dating back fifty years or more. They aren't necessarily valuable, but they make beautiful jewelry."

"My ex-wife only liked jewelry that cost a bundle."

"Oh, come on!" Surely the beauty of the object was what counted. "Maybe she just likes the look of pearls or precious stones."

"Nope. Unless it was hard on my wallet, it didn't count," he said. "It didn't start out that way. When we met, she was a dispatcher. Lively and fun to be around. A lot of guys wanted to date her, and it felt great that she'd chosen me. After we got married, things that hadn't bothered her before became a big issue."

"Like what?"

"My working overtime, putting in rotating shifts. I supposed the fault was partly mine. I didn't take her to dinner very often, didn't bring her flowers. Maybe she was lonely. After a while, whenever I drew an inconvenient shift or had to spend my day off in court testifying, the only way to pacify her was to buy her earrings or a bracelet."

"As a sign that you cared about her, surely."

"Partially," Mike conceded. "It was easier than fighting. We fell into a pattern—she threw a tantrum, I bought her off. Or anyway, it felt like I was buying her off. But let's not dwell on that." Mike caught her elbow to help her over a tumble of rocks that divided the small park from the quay. "Getting back to your glass collection, I didn't see any identifying information on the shadow boxes. With all this history, I would think you'd try to document it."

Paige was more than happy to return to that subject. "I got compulsive for a while, trying to label everything," she admitted. "Then I realized I'd stopped looking at the beauty of the glass, so I threw out all my notes."

His stride broke. "You threw them out?"

"Does that shock you?"

A hint of his citrus shaving lotion tickled her nose. "Kind of."

"You would never do that," Paige guessed.

"Throw away my hard work?" he returned. "Not without good reason."

"Losing touch with what's important *is* good reason," she said.

Mike started to answer, but apparently thought the better of it. "Interesting point of view," was all he said.

They reached the wooden quay that edged the harbor. Built on pilings over water, it anchored a series of small private piers that extended outward at right angles, securing sailboats, motorcraft and a few yachts. To their left, on the inland side, an array of shops offered swimwear and surfboards. Most were closed at this early hour except for one selling tackle and bait. Ahead, a few hardy fishermen perched along the public pier, lines trailing in the water.

"I wonder if they ever catch anything," Mike mused. "They seem to enjoy just sitting there."

"Aunt Bree once caught a halibut, or so she claimed." Paige suspected her aunt had bought it at a fish market, but she'd been too tactful to say so. In any case, it had tasted delicious. "She said she caught sole and turbot sometimes. And once a stingray."

"Ouch! What did she do with it?"

"Cut it loose, I presume." Even small rays could inflict nasty wounds.

"How do you treat a stingray injury, Doc?" Mike asked. "Any home remedies?"

Paige shuddered. "It's not like a jellyfish sting that you can sometimes get away with soaking in vinegar. With stingrays, there's a serious risk of shock and infection. As far as I know, there's no specific antidote to the toxin, but antibiotics and careful monitoring can usually mitigate the damage. Is this really what you want to discuss on a morning like this?"

"What I'd like to discuss is unfortunately confidential," Mike said. "Not that I couldn't use feedback."

"A case?"

"That's right."

Nearby, on the deck of the Sea Star Café, a few hardy

souls sat eating breakfast beneath heat lamps. A grizzled man was reading a newspaper, while a young couple and their toddler watched a pelican study their breakfast from a nearby post. A couple of seagulls circled noisily above, alert for crumbs.

"Isn't your brother getting back from his honeymoon today?" Paige asked. "Surely you could talk to him."

"This client would rather not involve my staff. Sensitive matter." His forehead furrowed. Whatever was going on clearly troubled him.

"Why don't we stop for a muffin?" Although Paige had eaten two slices of toast at the house, irresistible baking scents wafted from the café.

"I'm game."

They stepped into a cocoon of warmth amid the aromas of coffee, cinnamon, chocolate and apple. "Grab a table by the window," Paige said, not that they had much competition in the nearly empty café. "What would you like?"

"You have a seat. I'll get the food."

She fixed Mike with a stern look. "You are not in charge, Detective. I'm buying, so what'll you have?"

He chuckled. "You're a tough cookie."

"Would that be an oatmeal cookie or a chocolate chip cookie?" She could see both varieties displayed in a glass-topped plate on the front counter.

"Blueberry muffin and a cup of coffee."

"Done." She chose an apple fritter for herself, along with herb tea, and resisted the temptation to add a lemon tart. If she weren't careful, she'd balloon out like some of her patients. How many times had she blithely counseled them to moderate their weight gain? Only now did she understand the ferocity of their cravings.

As she waited for the barista to prepare the order, Paige studied Mike across the room. His thick, wind-tousled hair only added to his rugged impression, as did the watchfulness he maintained. Glancing out the window and then at the door seemed like second nature to him.

A memory haunted her. About a year and a half ago, she'd come here with a colleague she was dating at her old medical practice. Her mental image of Dr. Harry Myers made quite a contrast, with his pear-shaped build—narrow shoulders, heavy hips—and thinning hair. At the time, she'd found him attractive enough. They'd gotten along well, enjoying easy conversations and an uncomplicated relationship between equals.

Paige had begun to imagine a future for them, until Harry attended his twenty-year high school reunion and dropped her for his old girlfriend. Paige had found the atmosphere at work strained, especially after Harry showed up at a staff barbecue with his fiancée clinging to his arm, flashing a large diamond ring and giggling at his every word.

It had been a narrow escape, she supposed. She'd been so eager for a husband and a child that she'd been prepared to settle for a man who seemed simply good enough. In retrospect, she'd been more disappointed than wounded.

Now, if it were Mike...

Her jaw tightened. She didn't want to fall for this guy. Too hard-edged, too self-contained, too dangerous to her equilibrium. Thank goodness she knew in advance that they weren't suited.

When the barista called her name, Paige collected a fragrant tray and carried it to the table. Mike inhaled appreciatively. "That's my idea of heaven. A beautiful woman with a tray of food. And don't take that the wrong way. I'm not being sexist."

"The hell you aren't." She set the food down and took a seat. "But I'll forgive you this once."

They sorted out their drinks and goodies. After consuming a few bites, Mike leaned back. "I wish I knew why this case bothers me so much."

"Could you talk about it hypothetically?" Paige had occasionally solicited Bree's advice on the emotional aspects of cases by changing the details to protect the patient's privacy.

Mike didn't have to think for long. "Okay, here's the problem. If, or rather when, I tell this client what she asked me to find out, it might cause her to take action that could harm her."

"She's suicidal?" Paige guessed.

"No. She might confront someone she shouldn't touch with a ten-foot pole."

"Can't you warn her?" That seemed obvious.

"I can't be sure that will stop her." He drummed his blunt-tipped fingers on the table. "Also, something about the situation doesn't add up. I keep wondering what might be going on beneath the surface."

Having finished her apple fritter, Paige focused on Mike's concern rather than on the alluring array of baked goods across the room. "Doesn't your client want to know the whole truth?"

"Not necessarily. I've already found the answer to the question she asked me to research." He took a sip of coffee.

"But the more she understands, the better armed she'll be against this person, right?" Paige said.

His distant gaze came into sharp focus. "That's a good point. If she authorizes me to pursue the matter further, she isn't likely to take action in the meantime. And by then, she should have a better idea what she's up against. It seems obvious now that I hear it from you."

"All I did was reflect back what you were saying."

"You'd be surprised how rare it is to find someone who listens well."

"You don't have to tell me," Paige answered. "Some of my patients are starving for someone who'll pay attention."

"I thought women confided all their problems in their girlfriends." He cocked his head.

"Not everyone has close friends." *Especially when they work long hours and lose the one person they trusted most.* "Ideally, they'd be able to share with their husbands or boyfriends, but a lot of men have trouble opening up."

"I suppose you could say that about me." That was quite an admission, coming from Mike. "I grew up keeping my thoughts to myself."

"Your parents must be good at communicating. They'd have to be, to deal with all those foster kids," Paige said.

"They were great," he confirmed. "We had family councils, and any child who stayed more than a few weeks got professional therapy, which included sessions with my parents. Marianne and I were another story. We felt more like staff than kids."

She could imagine how that might happen. "Did you complain?"

"I just accepted the way things were." Mike stopped to observe a rowdy group of teenagers jostling each other in the doorway. He relaxed when they sorted themselves out and headed for the counter. "My sister and I were both affected, though. She's a dentist, like Dad, and unmarried, like me. I don't think either of us wants children."

"That must disappoint your parents." Her own parents

had adored each and every one of their numerous grand-children.

"Oh, my foster sister Lourdes has two kids, my brother Denzel has one and of course Lock and Erica are expecting."

Was that a note of hurt in his voice, that his parents lavished so much love on his siblings? "I'll bet they'd be surprised to learn how you feel. They may take you for granted, but the love for a child runs deep."

"I'm hardly a child now." He eyed their empty dishes and cups. "Ready to go?"

Not really, but the place had filled up and people were standing in line for tables. "Sure."

Outside in the brisk sea air, Paige wished impulsively for Mike to wrap a protective arm around her. Already, though, he seemed to be drawing into his private distance.

That retreat, following his self-disclosure, was under-standable. All the same, she missed that tender side of Mike. Now that she'd glimpsed his vulnerability, it was going to be harder than ever to hold him away.

But for her peace of mind, she had to.

Chapter Ten

From Harbor Bluff Drive, Mike could see only a sliver of the Hightowers' home, sheltered behind a white stucco wall draped with pink bougainvillea. He halted his car in front of the locked wrought-iron gate and announced himself over the speaker.

A moment later, the gate clicked open. He drove onto a concrete parking circle textured and tinted to resemble paving stones. The single-story white home sprawled atop a bluff, a few palm trees and a bird-of-paradise plant softening the classical pillars in front.

Gemma had emailed yesterday, changing the meeting place from his office to her home. Her husband would be attending a League of Cities meeting in Los Angeles this morning and, with almost no chance of his dropping in unexpectedly, she preferred the privacy.

As he got out of his sedan, Mike noted the pristine condition of the off-white paint as well as a new oak garage door with stained-glass windows. Expensive stuff for a real-estate broker struggling in a down market.

At the door, a maid in a gray-and-white uniform ushered him inside. They crossed a faux-marble entryway, went down a short hallway past a home office, and entered a large carpeted room set with velvety couches and silk cushions. On an end wall hung a giant TV.

Expansive windows overlooked a curving pool. Beyond it lay a lower bluff that held the Harbor View Hotel and, beyond that, the harbor where yesterday Mike and Paige had shared breakfast. While buildings obscured most of the quay, the two of them might have been briefly visible during their stroll had anyone been watching with binoculars.

"Coffee, Mr. Aaron?" the housekeeper asked.

"No, thank you."

"Mrs. Hightower, she be here in a minute." With a shadow of a smile, the woman departed.

Mike started to set his briefcase on a low table, changed his mind out of deference to the satin finish and put it on the floor. No wonder Gemma didn't want to risk losing this gorgeous place in a divorce. And no wonder Yelena Yerchenko coveted it, if that was indeed her motive.

The woman had no doubt visited, perhaps several times, as a guest at parties. According to his research, the escrow company owner had done considerable business with Roy's brokerage. Nothing unusual about that. In fact, they'd likely been acquainted for the better part of a decade, yet according to Mrs. Hightower, the affair had only been going on about a year. What had changed?

A shift in air pressure announced the arrival of the lady of the house. Wearing high heels and encased in a tight knit suit, her hair sleek in its chignon, Gemma Hightower entered with the carriage of someone making an entrance at the yacht club. Mike wondered if she was on her way to an event or if she dressed this way all the time.

Possibly both.

"Detective," she said by way of greeting. "What do you have for me?"

As Mike retrieved the folder from his case, she perched on the front of a chair, angling her long legs to one side like a model. She must have learned to do that during her days as a debutante in Virginia, where she'd grown up in a patrician family near Washington, D.C. Her father had been a mere bureaucrat, but her mother's family had a high social rank dating back to pre–Civil War days.

Mike researched his clients as well as their targets.

"Here's what I found." Seated on the couch, he presented photos along with his written report.

Holding them with her fingertips, Gemma turned pale. "That's Yelena. I never thought…" Swallowing hard, she thrust the shots back into the folder as if they burned. "Do I really need to read the report?"

"I'll sum it up for you. She lives near the restaurant, although, as you know, she owns a business here in Safe Harbor," Mike said. "I could stake out her house and shoot more images, but that hardly seems necessary."

Eyes dull with tears, Mrs. Hightower shook her head.

Now for the something extra that Paige had inspired. "I researched her background." Mike didn't need to consult notes for this part. "She's been in this country for about a dozen years and has permanent-resident status. Her permits and licenses appear to be in order."

"Why should I care about that?" Gemma asked crossly.

Mike described Yelena's knife attack on her former boyfriend. It had been mentioned in the newspaper, but without all the details. "In my opinion, she slashed him in a jealous rage and made it look like self-defense. I thought you might prefer to find some other way to dissuade her rather than a one-on-one confrontation."

Although he wouldn't have thought it possible, Gemma blanched even more profoundly. "Oh, Lord. You're right. If I had some way to…I don't like to use the word *blackmail*, but…I just did, didn't I?"

Mike pretended he hadn't heard. Blackmail was illegal. However, there was no law against giving someone reason to think twice about her actions. "I was considering avenues to explore and I wondered if she might have an ulterior motive for this affair. I don't have access to her financials beyond what's public record. However, there may be something in your husband's bank transactions that would give me a clue if they're working some sort of deals together. Something that could put her business at risk."

"Deals?" Mrs. Hightower bit down on her lips, turning them white against white.

"Are there large, unexplained deposits in any of his accounts?" Mike continued. "I wouldn't put it past Yelena to have come up with some scheme, given how tough things have been in real estate."

"A scheme?" The tears in her eyes seemed to freeze into ice crystals. "Don't you dare put my husband's business in jeopardy!"

"I'm just throwing out ideas." Mike should have realized that Mrs. Hightower wouldn't risk her financial security. "If you prefer, we could focus on Yelena. She still makes regular trips to Russia. Since as far as I could determine she has no family there, that raises interesting questions."

"Are you implying she has mob connections?"

He'd considered that possibility. But if she had ties to unsavory characters inside Russia, then by implication so did Roy Hightower. "Honestly, I haven't had time to move beyond a preliminary assessment. I just wanted to discuss options."

His client arose with remarkable smoothness on her spiky heels. "Well, Detective, I am exercising my options. This case is at an end. From here on, I will handle it my way."

He stood also. "That's your choice. However, you've paid for several more hours of my time. I'm happy to do the research."

"Keep the money."

Since the retainer was nonrefundable, he intended to do just that. "I hope I've provided everything you expected."

Tightly, she indicated the folder. "Unfortunately, yes. You've done very well. I don't mean to harp on this, but everything we've discussed is strictly confidential, isn't that so?"

"Yes, ma'am."

"You have no reason to go to anyone else with this information?"

"Absolutely not." Had he found evidence of illegal activities, Mike would be obligated to report it. But he hadn't, and regardless of any suspicions he might entertain, the probe stopped here.

When Mrs. Hightower shook his hand, hers felt boneless. "If we run into each other again, as I expect we will, you will give no sign that we have any particular acquaintance."

"Of course not."

He'd struck a nerve, Mike reflected as he exited into the June sunshine. Had it been the mention of large deposits?

Instincts honed as a police officer urged him to get to the bottom of this. But he had no right to do that. On the contrary, he had a duty to respect his client's privacy.

Vague suspicions didn't amount to evidence. While he feared that whatever was going on might blow up in the Hightowers' faces, that was their business, not his.

AFTER A JAM-PACKED MORNING when she worked in a couple of patients who'd suffered problems over the weekend,

Paige ate a sandwich at her desk while updating charts. She kept fighting itchy eyelids and incipient yawns, her body's annoying reminders that a nap would feel wonderful. Instead, she took extra vitamin supplements to make sure she wasn't becoming anemic, and forged onward.

Guiltily, Paige reflected that she ought to schedule her first maternity checkup with Dr. Rayburn. Since his office was next door, that shouldn't take much time, but for now she hated to spare even a few minutes. Now, if she could just focus on this chart...

Hearing a tap on her open door, she snapped to attention. Good heavens, had she dozed off without realizing it?

"Am I intruding?" Those sharp green eyes belonged to Nora Franco. With a surge of pleasure, Paige waved in her friend and colleague.

"You are totally welcome, anytime." She clicked shut the patient's records on the computer.

Her fellow obstetrician, wearing jeans and a flowing checkered top suitable for a nursing mom, took a chair. "You left the wedding in a hurry. I heard someone broke into your house. Sorry I didn't call sooner, but Neo caught a fever and I've been preoccupied."

"He's doing well now?"

"Right as rain. He's at my sister-in-law Kate's house, playing with his cousins. Everything okay at your place?"

Paige explained about the drunken party guest. "Mike Aaron was a big help. He boarded up the window that night while I was at the hospital."

"I hear he's renting a room from you." Nora regarded her archly. "Word spreads fast at the police department." Her husband, Leo, had taken over Mike's former job as a detective handling crimes against persons. Obviously, he knew the guys who'd stopped by to watch TV.

"Purely platonic," Paige assured her.

"I didn't ask."

"You didn't have to."

Nora's cheeks flushed. "Well, he ought to be reliable. Mike and Leo were never the best of friends, but Leo respects him. How's everything else?"

An innocuous question under normal circumstances, but the urge to confide about her pregnancy had intensified with each passing day. Paige had counseled Nora through her accidental pregnancy and ups and downs with Leo before their marriage. If anyone would empathize, it was her.

"I haven't told anyone yet, but I'm pregnant," Paige said, and inhaled sharply. Speaking the words aloud seemed to make it official.

Surprise and pleasure shaded to uncertainty in Nora's expression. "Is this a good thing? I didn't know you were seeing anyone."

"I'm not and yes, it's a good thing," Paige told her. "I had AI." That was medical shorthand for artificial insemination, although she'd mentioned the term once around a patient, a computer engineer, who'd asked in confusion why she should consider using artificial intelligence to get pregnant.

"Good for you!" Nora brightened. "You have guts. I considered it back when I didn't think I'd ever find Mr. Right, but going through motherhood alone was a scary prospect. I doubt my father knows one end of an infant from the other. My mom did all the infant care when I was little."

"I have a lot of family," Paige conceded, "but none of them live around here. Not since my aunt died."

"You must miss her a lot. I really liked her." During their residency, Nora had had dinner with Bree and Paige several times. "You aren't thinking of moving back to Texas, are you?"

"Not really." Not at all, yet Paige discovered she couldn't entirely dismiss the idea of all those loving arms and family gatherings to welcome her little one.

"Good!" Leaning forward, Nora folded her hands on the desk. "Remember what we discussed at the wedding?"

She'd mentioned returning to work, Paige recalled. "If you're ready to come back, I'd love to have you." The suite was large enough to accommodate two doctors, although they'd need to add another nurse.

"Seeing everyone last Saturday made me miss work. And I keep wondering what's happened to all my patients." Nora shook back her blonde hair, which looked thicker than ever. "It'll be hard to leave Neo, even though I think he'd enjoy the hospital day-care center. I hear it's excellent. Still, I'd only work part-time."

"When can you start?" The sooner the better.

"That's what I wanted to talk to you about."

How complicated could it be? Paige wondered. "Oh?"

Distractedly, Nora tugged on her maternity top. Her breasts must be filling up with milk, making her uncomfortable. "I'm presuming you'll continue working after you have your baby, right?"

"Of course." Paige couldn't afford to quit even if she wanted to, which she didn't. "I might cut back my hours for a few months, though."

"That's fine. Here's the thing." Nora drew a breath. What was she nervous about? "I'd like you to consider making this arrangement permanent by buying a half interest in my practice."

Paige's mind raced. She hadn't considered this possibility. From paying the ongoing expenses in the months since Nora went on leave, she had an idea of the operating costs, but no sense of what the practice might be worth. "How much did you have in mind?"

"We can have the practice appraised. When I bought it, it didn't cost much, honestly."

This was so unexpected, Paige had a hard time wrapping her mind around the idea. "I'm not sure I can afford it, with the baby coming."

"There are different ways to structure payments. You wouldn't have to come up with the whole amount at once." It sounded as if Nora had done her homework. Not too difficult, considering that her brother-in-law Tony Franco was the hospital's attorney and well versed on medical-related issues.

Paige supposed she could borrow the money, especially since she owned the house outright. While that would require making payments she hadn't figured into her budget, there would be advantages to part-ownership, including the security of knowing she couldn't be fired or have her hours cut. On the other hand, she'd be taking on a long-term commitment.

"We can work out a fair financial split if I'm only working part-time and you're basically full-time," Nora continued. "Of course we'll share a receptionist and support staff." The practice already divided the cost of clerks for records, billing and accounting with Dr. Rayburn, Paige had learned.

"I guess I just have one more question," she said. "Why are you so eager to do this?"

Nora paused before answering. "To make things more permanent and predictable. To know I can count on you. And frankly, Leo's a little concerned. Tony told him how much the patients love you and he got the idea you might leave to start your own practice and take them with you."

"I wouldn't do that!" Paige struggled not to take the comment as an insult. "That would be unethical."

"I didn't mean it that way. I know you'd never intentionally undercut me." Nora regarded her apologetically. "I just wanted you to hear everything so you don't feel later like I hid things from you."

Fair enough. "I understand. But I'll need to think about it."

"That's fine. Just remember that this would give you more control over your financial destiny. By the way, when are you due?"

"In February."

"That's wonderful! I'm glad you have Mike in the house in case you need help. Is he going to stay after the baby's born?" Nora waved away her own question. "I forgot. You haven't told him yet."

"He's only staying for the summer, anyway." Hearing the wistfulness in her voice, Paige added, "After that, I'll need the second bedroom for the baby."

She would have loved to chat further, but Keely's dour appearance in the doorway emphasized that personal discussions were at an end. "The next patient's prepped, Doctor."

"Thank you." Paige got to her feet.

"I'd like to start scheduling patients by mid-July. Mornings only. No surgery yet." Nora cleared her throat, obviously unwilling to say too much in front of the nurse. "Let me know what you decide. No rush."

"Absolutely."

Nora's proposition played through Paige's mind for the rest of the day. They hadn't discussed what would happen if Paige decided not to buy in. Would Nora replace her with another doctor willing to pay the price? Even if she didn't do so immediately, with her husband pressing the issue, she was likely to start looking. Given Safe Harbor's growing reputation, she'd have no trouble finding a taker.

Paige hadn't expected to have to make a choice like this, not with everything else going on. A few times, she felt a flare of anger, but she could hardly blame Nora, who hadn't even known about the pregnancy until today. And as long as they agreed on a reasonable price, Paige ought to be able to swing it.

She had no intention of leaving this area or Aunt Bree's beloved home. But this seemed so inflexible. What if she did decide she missed her family more than she'd imagined? With a baby on the way, she was seeing a lot of things afresh.

By the time Paige headed for home around 6 p.m., she felt as if she'd spent the day digging postholes and wrangling cattle. She'd stayed late to see Sheila and her recalcitrant husband, Gil, a pudgy fellow with a beer gut. Hard to figure how anyone could cheat with him while married to Mike. His condescending attitude hadn't endeared him, either, but perhaps he was keeping up his guard out of insecurity.

The man certainly appeared to be hiding his true motive. Paige got the impression Gil had deliberately refused to see her until after five in the expectation that she'd be unavailable. When that didn't work, he'd refused to give a sperm sample until he could see the renowned new head of the men's fertility program. Gil had read in the newspaper that Dr. Cole Rattigan would be arriving late in the year and, to his wife's disgust, refused to accept that Paige was competent to order the initial, routine testing. Only an expert in male fertility was good enough, one who wouldn't join the staff for months.

She'd waited until Gil boxed himself completely into a corner before saying sweetly, "Fortunately, Dr. Rattigan's schedule has changed and we expect him in July. I'll make sure he works you in right away."

Displeasure had yielded to reluctant acquiescence, and she'd made the referral. After her husband stepped out, Sheila had thanked Paige earnestly. "I know he's being stubborn, but he really does want kids. It's just that doctors intimidate him."

"Don't forget about counseling. He might be uncomfortable with the idea of giving sperm, or there could be something else bothering him."

"I mentioned it, but he's not interested."

At least he'd agreed to see Dr. Rattigan. Hopefully, they'd soon have test results and could proceed from there

The visit had sapped what little energy Paige retained. After eating a quick meal at the cafeteria, she drove home on fumes.

As she pulled up, she felt a tug of irritation. In front of her house the shaggy-looking man leaned against her low fence, smoking and drinking beer. Discarded cigarette butts littered her patio and when he spotted her, his face creased smugly.

Paige parked in the garage and got out, trying to decide on her next move. Call the police? She wasn't sure loitering qualified as a crime, or that it was worth troubling them about.

Then Mike's silver sedan pulled into her driveway. Climbing out, he lifted a hand in greeting and turned to face the interloper.

In a business suit, with an ink smudge on his jaw, he didn't exactly resemble a knight in shining armor. But he came the closest Paige had seen in a long time.

Chapter Eleven

Ceding the defense of her home to anyone else went against the grain. Yet today, Paige watched gratefully as Mike, with only the tightening of his fists betraying his tension, calmly addressed the intruder. "Doesn't drinking beer violate your parole, Willy?"

At the sound of his name, the gray-haired man jerked so hard he dropped the can. Paige smelled the yeasty brew as it ran into the storm drain. "Now look what you made me do!" the man complained. "How'd you know my name, anyway?"

"Willy Kerrigan. You held up a liquor store for a couple of hundred dollars and two six-packs of beer to pay for your drug habit," Mike said. "I can fill in the details of your parole, if you like."

"You got no right to snoop on me!" The man's jaw thrust forward.

"I'm a private detective. Snooping is what I do. Anything else you'd rather I didn't find out?"

It took Willy only a moment to grasp the implication that pressure would simply make things worse. Giving his head a taut shake, he scooped up the can. "You gonna report me?"

"Only if you keep harassing my housemate," Mike said levelly.

"You're living here?" Annoyance flickered over the man's ferretlike features. "Okay. I'm leaving, see?" He turned away.

"You forgot something." When the man glanced back, Mike indicated the cigarette butts on the sidewalk.

Lip curling, Willy picked them up. He started to toss them into the gutter, saw a sign warning against putting anything except water in storm drains, and carried them all the way to the halfway house.

Mike hadn't even raised his voice.

"Impressive," Paige said. "Thanks."

"I consider policing the grounds part of my duties as a tenant," Mike told her as they went inside.

"Good to remember. I'll be sure to put it in the lease." Not that she'd given him a lease, although no doubt she ought to.

In the living room, Paige collapsed onto the couch. "Rough day," she explained. "Usually I prefer to fight my own battles, but I'm glad you were there."

"So am I." He stowed his laptop case in a corner, shrugged off his jacket and dropped into an oversize chair. The open collar of his blue shirt revealed a lightly tanned throat and shadowed jawline. "Seems to me men and women tend to complement each other. Different talents, different strengths. Dividing up the responsibilities makes life easier."

"He-men take out the trash and bonk the burglars, and she-women wear frilly aprons and knead the bread dough?" Paige asked warily.

Her parents had divided up their responsibilities, but it had come at the price of her mother's avocation as a photographer. Birdy—a nickname she'd preferred to her real name, Bertha—had quit shooting family events in deference to her husband, who liked being in charge of picture-taking. The result was scrapbooks full of poorly composed and over- or underexposed photos that even computer software couldn't fix.

"I've got a woman detective who can bonk burglars with the best of them. But I don't object to frilly aprons, with as little as possible underneath." Mike tilted his head as if awaiting Paige's riposte.

Once, she might have bristled. Instead, she chuckled. "You're irrepressible."

"That's good, right?"

"Depends on my mood." She fixed him with what she hoped was a piercing look. "And don't tell me women are moody."

"No more than men," he agreed. "It's fine to get angry as long as you're up front about it. What I can't stand is the way my ex-wife hid her anger, then did sneaky things to get back at me."

"For instance?"

"Claiming she'd bought something I needed at the store and then, when it was too late for me to stop off on the way home, suddenly claiming she forgot."

"That's petty," she said.

"And she cheated on me," he added sardonically.

With a man who doesn't come close to measuring up to you, as far as I can tell. "Which was worse?" Paige asked, only half joking.

"Running out of potato chips." He gave a dry laugh. "Let's talk about something more pleasant. Anything interesting happen today?"

"The doctor I'm filling in for asked me to buy a partnership in the practice." She described Nora's offer. "It's tempting but every time I started to say yes, I felt this wall of resistance. I'm not sure why."

"Owning your own business is a big step." Mike rose

from the chair. "Before we go into that topic, care for something to drink? There's wine."

Delicious as that might taste, alcohol could harm her baby. "Orange juice would be great."

"You got it." He returned a minute later with the refreshing drink, and sat down to discuss the pros and cons of business ownership. Mike offered insight from experience, especially about the curse of red tape. Nevertheless, according to him, being your own boss more than outweighed the downside.

Paige had missed having a sounding board, she realized. Whenever something was weighing on her mind, Aunt Bree used to listen and offer feedback. Sometimes, the mere act of airing her thoughts aloud made the right choice obvious.

While she wasn't ready to make a decision in this instance, Mike's responses helped clarify her thinking. Yes, she wanted to buy into the practice, except for one problem. She longed to provide her baby with a large, loving family, and that meant moving back to Texas.

Warm, smothering family. Lots of love, lots of advice and lots of interference. But Paige had been gone for years except for brief visits. Perhaps old relationships could be reestablished on a fresh basis.

That would require leaving this delightful house with its precious memories, along with her friends and patients at Safe Harbor. Paige wished she could talk this part over with Mike, too, but that would require disclosing her pregnancy. And while she had to tell him soon, not tonight.

"I'd be happy to refer you to my lawyer and accountant," Mike was saying. "It's a good idea to have an independent eye review the paperwork."

"I'd appreciate that."

"I'll email the information to you tomorrow."

"Great." Paige sprang up to put their glasses in the sink, and discovered that she didn't feel tired anymore. "How about a swim?"

He glanced toward the window. "It's getting dark."

"All the more fun. I don't dare swim at night by myself." The ocean presented challenges that even on a routine day ranged from undercurrents to jellyfish, and the city's lifeguards knocked off at five.

"Oh, danger!" Mike said cheerily. "What are we waiting for?"

She should have known he'd go for the daredevil aspect. "Last one into the water has to fix breakfast."

"With our clothes on?" He sounded ready to go for it.

"After we've changed." Laughing, Paige headed for her bedroom.

Stripping off her work clothes, she tied on the daring emerald bikini that had made such an impression on Mike the last time he saw it. Pausing to examine her long, slim figure in the mirror, she saw no sign yet of a bulge. Might as well wear the bikini while she could.

She slung a thin strap around her waist, holding a watertight pouch for her key and ID. From the hall linen closet, she grabbed a couple of large towels and hurried into the living room. Mike hovered near the front door, his strong body bare above a pair of red trunks. Heat invaded Paige as she took in his toned chest and narrow waist. To cover her reaction, she tossed him a towel. "That's for you."

He slung it over his shoulders. "Thanks. I figured I'd air-dry on the walk home, but this is better."

When she opened the door, her hot body relished the coolness. "That feels good."

Mike waited while she set the alarm and locked the door. Then he raised his towel like a banner. "Waffles and scrambled eggs. That's what I'd like when you cook my breakfast." Off he shot.

Paige flew forward, glad she'd worn sneakers. Her muscles relished the challenge, and even though Mike had a brief head start, she caught up with him at the intersection with Seaside Lane as he waited for a truck to pass.

They crossed to the beach, empty now of the day's sunbathers. Ahead, a lingering sunset layered the heavens with cerise and gold against deepening blue. Feeling as if she could fly into that gorgeous sky, Paige pelted over the sand, barely pausing to kick off her shoes and pitch her towel in a heap.

The prospect of beating Mike to the water energized her. While he had the advantage of longer legs, she had more experience gaining traction in the sand, and splashed into the swirl of tidewater first.

"Beatcha!" Paige called, pressing forward through the cool water. As the sand sloped underfoot, she took off swimming.

"Worth it!" Mike cut through a low swell to arrive beside her. "You look great from the back."

"Waffles, eggs *and* sausage!" she returned, and dove into an oncoming wave.

In the silence beneath the water, she lost track of Mike until he cut under her and surfaced, lifting her on his back and tumbling her into the water again. Paige doubled around like a playful seal and pushed him. Their hips grazed and their legs tangled, and then she swam off. He caught up easily and bumped her in turn.

The next thing she knew, they were somersaulting through the waves, tickling and rolling over each other. His movements adapted easily to hers, as if he could read her intentions, but she got in her share of bumps and nudges.

During a glancing frontal contact, there was no mistaking a hard masculine part of him. Paige knew she ought to quit now, but as her feet found the shallow sandy floor, she couldn't resist running her hands over the toned muscles on Mike's chest. She registered every taut fiber of him as his arms captured her waist and his mouth relished hers. Pressing into him, her breasts felt on fire, while her core ached for fulfillment.

Stepping away, Paige struggled to catch her breath. "Maybe we'd better take this indoors."

"My thought exactly."

He drew her out of the surf. Without speaking, they collected their towels and sandals.

This was Mike, the man who for an entire year she'd considered too macho and rough-edged. Suddenly, Paige was sharing her house with him, and now…

She refused to think beyond the moment. Everything in her cried out for satisfaction, and why not?

She made her own decisions and took the consequences. Right now, Paige wanted the pure joy of being held and loved, even though it couldn't last.

She strode home beside Mike, covering the ground almost as fast as when they'd been racing.

FOR MONTHS, MIKE HAD BEEN fantasizing about Paige. Given her stubborn independence, he'd figured she would be the one to call it quits tonight when they started getting physical. Instead, she seemed eager and willing as they paced up the sidewalk to her cottage.

Terrific. He'd been ready for an entire year.

If a few concerns tried to raise their ugly heads—pesky reminders of how mismatched expectations and conflicting dreams could wreck relationships—he hammered them down. Let the future take care of its damn self.

How could he resist toweling off her long thick hair, dark auburn and shiny with dampness? In the living room, Mike drew the towel around them both, smoothing the long, plush lines of her waist and breasts, lifting off that sexy bikini top and rubbing the towel across her erect nipples.

Paige hooked her thumbs into the waist of his trunks and tugged him to her bedroom. He'd imagined this scene a hundred different ways this past week, but the reality was unbelievably superior. The velvet of her skin. The hunger in her mouth. The tantalizing light in her eyes as she lowered the trunks over his hips.

Mike had to rein in his need while he retrieved a condom from his room. Returning to find that she'd tossed aside the blue quilt, he drew on the protection, fumbling a couple of times until she reached over and smoothed it on with the skilled fingers of a surgeon.

Heart thundering, he untied the strip of bikini that guarded her secrets. She was beautiful everywhere, just as he'd pictured her. Lowering Paige to the bed, he savored the moment, arousing her with his mouth until she caught his shoulders and pulled him onto her. Even then, he struggled to enter her cautiously until fire flashed over him and seared away all restraint.

Glory raging through him, Mike drove into her, treasuring her gasps of desire, until he stopped to catch his breath. In a flash, Paige rolled him over and took him in her own fashion, breasts and stomach shining with moisture. They tussled again as they had in the surf, tumbling and thrusting, waves washing over and through him until Mike forgot everything except the thrilling crest of pleasure.

As joy faded to a glow, he lay beside her, astonished. Mike had never lost control before, never lost the awareness of himself as a separate being. Not like this.

Drawing the covers over them, Paige rested her cheek on his shoulder. Damp hair brushed his neck. "That was incredible."

"For me, too." Holding her, Mike relaxed into the memory of all that splendor. He'd like to do it again, soon.

Despite his intention, his body seemed content to lie here peacefully beside her. After a while, her steady breathing told him she'd drifted into sleep.

Mike wasn't ready to doze off. He had computer work to do, and needed to set his alarm to get to work in the morning. Reluctantly, he eased away, careful not to disturb Paige.

How splendid she looked, the covers revealing a generous expanse of hair and breasts. He'd been a little concerned that if they became lovers, living together might throw them too much in each other's way. But he'd run that risk, gladly.

Humming under his breath, Mike went to take a shower.

PAIGE COULD HARDLY BELIEVE they'd made love in Bree's bedroom. Yet the glimmer of purple glass on the bureau seemed to say that her aunt approved. After all, Bree had been no prude.

Although she missed waking up beside Mike, he was only down the hall, and later that night, they made love again. For the next few weeks, they continued to explore each other whenever the pair of them had a few hours free at the same time. Sometimes they used his bed, and once the living room sofa, but that proved too cramped, given their heights.

It was fun having him to play with, to share experiences, to take walks on the beach. Evening swims became a regular indulgence to wash off the cares of the day before plunging happily into their private intimacy.

Every now and then, Paige reminded herself that she ought to tell him about the pregnancy, but what was the rush? Her first prenatal checkup found everything progressing normally, and morning sickness hadn't troubled her as much as it did some patients.

While she'd gained a few pounds, Mike didn't seem to notice. No one else at work knew, either, except for Dr. Rayburn, his nurse Lori and Nora, who dropped by occasionally to ease her transition to work. She didn't press the partnership issue, thank goodness.

You can't go on keeping secrets. One world with Mike, another shared with the tiny creature inside her body as it took shape millimeter by millimeter, and then her public persona as a take-charge physician serving her patients. The worlds were bound to collide and Paige intended to soften the impact before it happened.

A deadline presented itself: his family's upcoming beach picnic to celebrate Independence Day. Paige didn't want to risk being outed by some sharp-eyed family member, such as Mike's mother, who'd experienced two pregnancies of her own, or perhaps Erica, who might get suspicious after seeing Paige in a swimsuit. Even a subtle disguise such as a one-piece instead of the bikini was likely to raise questions from Mike.

She meant to break the news the weekend before the holiday, but he had to put in extra-long hours on a case. Seeing his exhaustion when he arrived home, Paige shied away from holding such a serious conversation. *Before Saturday, I'll find the time.*

On Tuesday morning, however, she put her personal

concerns aside while performing a tubal anastomosis on a woman to reopen her fallopian tubes. The patient had undergone surgical sterilization during a previous marriage, and now needed to have it reversed to start a family with her second husband.

Dr. Tartikoff had taught Paige the microsurgical procedure. It required a special microscope and tools that enabled her to use extremely tiny stitches to hold the reconnected tissues.

"You're getting damn good at that," said Dr. Zack Sargent, who'd asked to assist her. A couple of new surgical fellows took up most of Dr. T's teaching time these days, leaving other doctors to coach each other on the procedures they'd learned.

"Thanks. She has two boys and longs for a girl, and her husband would be thrilled either way," Paige remarked as she worked. "So, what's up with your plans for a fertility scholarship? Are most of the doctors on board?"

"Hard to tell. That hundred thousand dollars is a big deal and most of them don't want to commit with nearly six months to go." Zack's discouraged expression drew a sympathetic glance from surgical nurse Stacy Raditch, a sweet young woman who made no secret of her attraction to the broad-shouldered widower. Zack never seemed to notice the longing gazes that followed him even in unflattering operating scrubs with a cap covering his thick dark-blond hair. Paige, while she liked her fellow obstetrician, found him too earnest for her taste.

"How're you doing in the race so far?" A chart in the doctors' lounge tracked the number of qualifying pregnancies attributed to each physician. Paige hadn't paid much attention, since she had little prospect of winning, but she'd noticed Dr. Tartikoff and Dr. Rayburn tied for the lead.

"Middling," he replied. "But that should change once the egg donor program takes off. I've concentrated my efforts on refining the techniques for harvesting eggs and transferring embryos." Due to Zack's enthusiasm for the planned program, Dr. T had agreed to let him work closely with the new director once she arrived.

"Any word on when Ms. Garcia will get here?" Dr. Tartikoff had hired an administrative nurse he'd formerly worked with in Boston. Jan Rios Garcia, who had a master's in molecular genetics, was now assistant director of an egg donor program in Houston. Her arrival had been delayed by contractual obligations.

"Latest word is September." Zack broke off to pose a question about the current procedure, which Paige answered in detail, since she was teaching him as well as performing the operation.

"Didn't Ms. Garcia used to work in L.A.?" Stacy asked when silence fell again. "I heard there was some problem at the hospital there."

Zack narrowed his eyes at her. "Let's keep gossip out of it."

The nurse blinked in surprise at his sharp tone. "Sorry, Doctor." She lowered her head as if hiding tears.

Zack's expression softened. "I didn't mean to snap. The truth is, I used to work with Jan. In fact, since it's bound to come out, we were engaged. I made the mistake of believing some unfounded accusations that were made against her. By the time I learned the truth, it was too late." He paused and for a moment Paige thought he might disclose more, but all he said was, "That was a long time ago. I'm hoping we can work together smoothly."

"Surely she wouldn't have accepted this position if she felt uncomfortable being around you," Paige pointed out.

Zack blew out a breath that ruffled his surgical mask.

"I'm not sure she knows I'm here. I'm not officially part of the program yet, and we haven't been in touch."

"You think she'll hold a grudge?"

"Not exactly. I suppose it might be more politic for me to try to find a comparable program elsewhere, but I'm not willing to uproot my daughter. She's had enough turmoil in her life."

"She's a sweetheart. You two were so cute dancing together at the wedding," Paige said.

"Much as I regret what happened with Jan, I can't be sorry I've become Berry's father," Zack responded.

"I'm sure it will work out." Romances among staff members created tension when they fell apart, as Paige had learned at her last practice. Still, a long time had obviously passed since Zack's involvement with Jan Garcia. "Is she married?"

"I haven't paid attention to her personal life." His tone made it clear the subject was closed.

September. When Jan Garcia arrived, would Paige still be here? She couldn't imagine leaving these people and places so soon, yet if Nora decided to press the matter of buying into the practice, Paige might be forced to make a quick decision. Of course, she could join another practice in the area, but that would be awkward while she was dealing with the pregnancy. And then, if she lost Mike…

Of course you're going to lose him. She couldn't expect a guy who didn't want children to hang around after she brought a baby home. Sleepless nights, hours of crying and postpartum hormone swings took their toll on even the most compatible couples.

Mike would vanish with a flash of the suitcase and the rumble of a borrowed truck. No wonder she kept putting off telling him.

After closing the patient and removing her scrubs,

Paige was halfway to the elevator when the sight of a towering and dearly familiar shape startled her. Mike hadn't mentioned anything about meeting her for lunch.

"Hi." She gave him a quizzical look. "It's nice to see you, but what brings you to the hospital?"

"Any reason I shouldn't stop by?" he countered.

Despite his light tone, the evasive answer bothered her. Mike was usually so direct. "Are you here to see me?"

"Just passing by."

No one just passed by the second floor, since there were no regular patient rooms here. She'd seen him at the bulletin board before the wedding, Paige recalled. Initially, she'd believed he was posting a notice about the bridal couple, but that hadn't turned out to be the case. Instead, he'd spotted her ad for a roommate—but he had never mentioned why he was there.

"Mike, what's going on?" Surely if he had a health issue, he'd have told her. Besides, none of the second-floor facilities involved treating male disorders.

He swallowed. As she waited, it occurred to Paige that she might not be the only one in this relationship keeping secrets.

But what his might be, she hadn't a clue.

Chapter Twelve

He should have paid more attention to Paige's schedule, Mike reflected, irked at his carelessness. He knew perfectly well she performed surgery right down the hall on Tuesdays, because he'd run into her before. Since then, he'd switched his regular visits to Wednesdays but, preoccupied with a case, he'd stopped by today without thinking.

If he invented an excuse or avoided answering, that would create friction. Also, since he'd already informed his family, this hardly qualified as a secret.

"I'm a donor." He tried not to squirm. Nothing to fuss about, especially given her profession.

"You're…" Paige frowned "…a regular sperm donor?"

"Is there some other kind?" He'd much rather talk about meeting for dinner tonight and squeezing in some alone time. A client's problem was going to cost him most of his free evenings this week, especially since he had to clear Saturday for the family picnic, but he didn't want to miss connecting with Paige.

She took a deep breath. "As a matter of fact, yes. Targeted donors provide sperm for a specific couple. For instance, Dr. Tartikoff did that for his brother and sister-in-law. Then they decided to use a surrogate without his knowledge and, well, things didn't go exactly as planned."

She smoothed back the dark red hair clipped at the nape of her neck. "That's a long story you don't need to hear."

"Then why are you telling me?" Because she was nervous, obviously. But why?

Paige cleared her throat. "How long have you been doing this?"

"Since April."

"April?"

"You know, the month that comes before May." Mike hoped her reaction didn't mean she expected to control this aspect of his life.

"Sorry. It's taking me a minute to wrap my head around this." She hesitated a moment before asking, "What inspired you to become a donor?"

"Egotism. Altruism. Pride. Good genes." Plus a fascination he couldn't explain, and didn't intend to try. "You're a doctor. You get the picture."

"But you don't want kids," she blurted.

"I don't want to *raise* kids," Mike corrected. "What's the big deal?" His position shouldn't require defending.

"Do you have a master's degree?" Paige asked out of the blue.

"Yes. In criminal science." This conversation was growing weirder by the minute. "What does that have to do with anything?"

"Nothing." She gave an apologetic wave. "I'm a little light-headed. I got so caught up in surgery, I didn't notice how hungry I was."

"Can you eat while operating?" He fell into step beside her en route to the elevator. "I mean, if you noticed you were hungry, what would you do?"

"In complex cases, doctors stay at it for hours and, yes, you eat. You're the lord of the operating room. If you need a snack, someone fetches it for you. Sticks it in your mouth if necessary so you don't contaminate your gloves." Paige seemed glad to seize on a neutral topic, which was fine with Mike.

Also, the subject interested him. "The blood and guts don't bother you?"

"Oh, I'd step away from the operating table. I wouldn't want to drop taco sauce into an incision." She shook her head. "That's not what you asked. Does the sight of blood turn my stomach? No. If it did, I'd leave surgery to someone else."

"You enjoy cutting people?" It seemed an odd choice for a woman who disliked boiling little sea creatures to collect their shells.

"In high school biology, when the other girls squealed about having to dissect a frog, I couldn't wait to find out what was inside. The only bad part was that the frogs had been killed in order to educate us. I wanted to help, not harm."

This was the kind of intriguing conversation Mike had come to expect from his flame-haired goddess. Thank goodness she'd moved past her reaction to his news. While many women might be taken aback by the idea of their lover fathering children with others, Paige was an obstetrician. With a little more reflection, no doubt she'd be cheering him on.

Alone with her in the elevator, Mike stole a quick kiss. "How about I pick up Italian food tonight? We can eat on the patio now that it's quiet again." Last week's renters, a noisy bunch of young men, had been followed this week—mercifully—by two elderly couples whose loudest activity consisted of playing dominoes near an open window. In addition, Willy had made himself scarce, although Mike was keeping an eye on a halfway house newbie who took too much interest in the contents of parked cars.

"Can't wait," Paige responded. When the doors opened, she cast a vague smile in his direction and strode down a hall toward the doctors' entrance.

Mike paused to watch the sway of her hips. The woman was stunning from every angle.

Telling her about his donations had been a good thing. With that out of the way, he saw clear sailing ahead until the end of summer and beyond. Far beyond, if he had any say in the matter.

TOO RESTLESS TO EAT IN THE cafeteria, Paige carried a sandwich to her office in the adjacent building. She'd barely kept a grip on her thoughts after Mike dropped that bomb on her. Thank goodness he hadn't realized how evasive she was being, because she was not prepared to deal with the possibilities his disclosure had raised.

With the door shut, she logged into the computer and accessed her chosen sperm donor profile. Height: check. Education: check. Coloring: check. That wasn't proof, and even if it had been possible to run a DNA test this early, she'd never invade Mike's privacy by stealing a sample.

On the sperm bank's password-protected site, Paige searched the other donor profiles. No one else matched so many parameters. Beyond any reasonable doubt, Mike was the father of her baby.

Out of all those men, she'd chosen him. How ironic was that? And how unbelievably awkward.

She'd experienced a similar sensation once in high school when the gym teacher pressured her into trying out for basketball and another girl body-slammed her. Paige had lain on the wooden floor gasping for breath, her entire body feeling squashed to about an inch thick.

Now, deep in her brain, she heard the voice of a surgeon under whom she'd trained. Stumped when an operation unexpectedly went south, he'd called out, "Options!" He'd been seeking the surgical team's input in a fierce attempt to save the patient's life. And together they had, miraculously, hit on a solution.

Paige wished she could shout "Options!" now, or at least had a friend to help her cut through the tangle of conflicting emotions. In the past few weeks she'd begun to rely on Mike to fill that role. Mike, the last person on earth she could consult now. This was too touchy to share even with Nora, especially since the outcome might affect Paige's decision about buying into the practice.

She'd have to serve as her own team. Bracing for action, she opened a file in the computer.

Option one: tell Mike he's going to be a dad.

Out of the question. He'd flee, and she'd miss him terribly. It was too soon to say good-bye.

Maybe it was selfish to keep him in the dark. But revealing the truth would put him into an unfair position. The man rejected fatherhood. He'd been scrupulous about using contraception during their lovemaking, and had sacrificed his marriage to Sheila over that matter.

Also, simply because he had the right to walk out on Paige didn't mean he'd get off scot-free. He'd spend the rest of his life knowing he'd fathered a baby with a woman he'd been close to. He might even see their child around town, if she chose to stay. That had to affect him, no matter how much he pretended otherwise.

Paige needed another possibility.

Option two: tell him and leave Safe Harbor. That had the merit of frankness, but it failed to address her other concerns. Besides, Paige didn't want to be forced to abandon her house and her patients. If she chose to return to Texas, it ought to be for positive reasons.

Option three: admit she was pregnant, and pretend

the father was a man no longer in the picture. But how could she account for the man's complete absence and for switching her attention so quickly to Mike? Paige refused to claim a casual encounter with a stranger. She'd never do that. Also, she was a lousy liar, which ruled out option three completely.

Option four: …was there an option four?

Yes. Break up with him. But what reason could she give? He'd see right through a trumped-up excuse and, anyway, that brought her back to being a lousy liar.

And to longing to enjoy every possible minute with him. Paige pictured Mike lying in her bed this morning, covers draped across his chest, his invigorating citrus scent filtering through every cell in her body. She yearned for more of his company, no matter how doomed the relationship might be in the long run.

Option five: delay telling him she was pregnant until she came up with a better idea.

If only she didn't have to face his entire family this weekend and pretend there was nothing amiss. She'd meant to disclose her pregnancy before then, but she supposed that had better wait until her next step became clear. She sighed. Option five won by default.

From down the hall, Paige heard Keely's voice as she took a patient's medical history. Duty called. Quickly, she deleted the file containing her options. Didn't need the reminder, anyway.

Aunt Bree used to advise her to live more in the present and less in the future. Once again, her aunt had been right.

MIKE HATED TO DISAPPOINT a client. Especially his biggest, most lucrative account—Kendall Technologies.

On Thursday, he pulled into the industrial complex

on the east side of town. Spotting his windshield pass, a guard waved him on between rows of palm trees into a parking lot enlivened by beds of purple petunias and yellow marigolds.

In these sprawling, low-rise buildings, engineers developed medical and surgical implants and other devices under the close supervision of founder and chief executive Officer Reese Kendall, a multimillionaire in his early forties. In addition to the manufacturing facilities here in Safe Harbor, Reese had opened a plant in Phoenix, Arizona.

Until the past few weeks, Mike's services to the company had focused on screening job applicants, reviewing security measures and looking into employee thefts of tools and occasionally the devices. Easy, routine work, with the occasional minor surprise to keep things interesting.

Now, laptop case in hand and discomfort dogging his steps, Mike cut across the lot to the administration building. Despite his and Lock's best efforts, he hadn't been able to identify the source of a major security breach.

This went far beyond the usual type of problem because it involved the theft of a prototype medical tool. A company in Russia had unveiled an identical product that, according to Kendall, couldn't have been developed purely by chance because of built-in proprietary information not disclosed to outside parties.

"If they can steal this, what's next?" Reese had asked when he brought Mike in. "We're working on a portable scanner that could revolutionize medical treatment. I can't afford to let this leak go unplugged, but if we bring in the FBI, they'll disrupt our business, scare our customers and endanger our security clearances. I want to know who's doing this and how."

Mike had been thorough. Painstaking. Abrasive, where necessary. He'd performed complete background checks not only on the engineers and executives who might have had official access to the information, but also the cleaning crews and clerical staff. He'd searched for any fired or otherwise disgruntled employees and hired as a consultant a P.I. who specialized in computer forensics to look for evidence of hacking into the computer system. Financial records of individuals had been scrutinized as per waivers they'd signed prior to employment. At every step, he'd kept Reese apprised of the progress, or lack of it.

In the plush pastel lobby, he passed scrutiny from another guard, and took the elevator to Reese's third-floor office. He'd missed his calling, Mike mused with a touch of envy as he took in the original glass artwork that transformed the hallway into a wonderland of shimmering hues and shapes. In a thousand years, a detective wouldn't earn enough to afford a place like this.

His envy faded. Big facility, big problems. Small office, small problems. Though perhaps not so small if he lost his top client.

Rounding a corner, he caught sight of Reese's secretary, a gray-haired woman wearing thick glasses who'd been personally selected by the CEO's second wife. Persia Kendall was a former executive trainee who'd stolen him from his first wife, Nora Kendall—now Nora Franco. Obviously, Persia took no chances on being supplanted in turn.

"Mr. Aaron. Good. I'll tell him you've arrived," the secretary said, half rising from her desk.

"No need. I'm here." Her boss sprang through the open doorway, hand outstretched. From his expensively cut dark hair to his designer silk suit, Reese Kendall might have stepped from the pages of a men's magazine, except for the worry lines creasing his forehead.

As they shook hands, Mike's gaze slid to a sculpted wooden wall clock. He was five minutes early. He'd never seen Reese this anxious.

And I have nothing to report.

That wasn't entirely true. Mike had some suggestions, but no conclusions. If he didn't solve this soon, there'd be no choice but to notify the authorities. That meant a broad-based search of the company's operations, exactly what Reese had hired him to prevent.

Inside, the office sprawled across an expanse larger than Paige's entire house. A parquet conference table dominated one side, while a gleaming kitchenette offered equipment that, aside from the fragrant espresso maker, Reese probably never bothered to use.

The CEO waved Mike into a leather armchair. "What've you got for me?"

"I'd like to review the measures I've already advised you on so you can understand the context…"

"Skip it. The context of what?" Reese's bright blue eyes, no doubt augmented by contact lenses, fixed on Mike.

This might not go over well, but it was all he had left. "As you know, I haven't yet identified the leak. That means either someone's hiding a financial connection that you'd need law-enforcement capabilities to access…"

"Don't tell me that." Reese ran a hand through his thick hair, leaving it uncharacteristically messy. "What else?"

"Or someone normally above suspicion is involved. Someone who might have walked out of here with the information on a laptop."

The CEO swiveled his chair sharply. "Tell me this isn't going where I think it is."

Mike kept his tone smooth. "Your chief engineer, Doug Loughlin, recently relocated to the Phoenix facility."

Reese shook his head. "Doug's been with me from the beginning. He owns a share in the company. Small, but worth a fortune. At thirty-eight, the man's rich enough to retire, but he loves to work. And he relocated to our own branch, to be near his wife's family. He didn't leave for another firm."

Best to keep the focus narrow. "Is it possible he had the designs for the prototype on his laptop?"

"Yes, but it's securely encrypted. You know the lengths we've gone to."

"Unfortunately, yes."

"Unfortunately because that means Doug stole them on purpose and sold them overseas?" Reese started to twist his subtly interwoven amber-and-blue tie, then released it quickly.

"Or he left the laptop turned on around someone he trusted. A family member. Personal cleaning staff."

"You think his maid downloaded a complicated piece of technology while he was in the bathroom? Sounds preposterous, but I suppose it's worth investigating."

"Already did." Mike handed over a printout. "She's worked for them ten years and she and her family moved with them to Phoenix. No questionable associations or financial transactions that I can find."

Reese barely glanced at the paper before dropping it on the desk. "Who else, then?"

"I'm asking your permission to contact Mr. Loughlin and request his cooperation." This would be tricky. No matter how carefully Mike phrased that conversation, he was likely to antagonize the man.

"I can't afford to lose Doug. It's insulting to question his integrity, and pointless."

Mike had run smack into a brick wall. "You hired me to make suggestions, and I'm making them."

On his feet now, Reese paced across the carpet. "Doug's as security conscious as I am. He was furious when he learned about the theft. He called me a couple of times, trying to figure out who on his staff might have done it. I gave you that information."

"And I followed up on it, as you'll see in my report. Drew a blank."

"I don't see how anyone could have stolen this information from him. We bend over backward to be discreet with our top people. When they're relocating, they don't even hold open houses to sell their homes. We guarantee the sale and take care of the whole process. Purchasers visit by appointment only, and always with our Realtor present."

Mike missed whatever Reese said next, because the words "Realtor" got stuck in his brain. Could that be the connection?

"Who handles the real estate transactions?" he asked.

"Mayor Hightower. He's a close friend as well as someone I respect professionally. In fact, I've been encouraging him to run for the state assembly," Reese answered. "Why?"

Although Mike had sometimes seen apparently unrelated threads weave together in an investigation, this was the first time it had happened—or potentially happened—since he'd left the police department. "Does he have a key to the homes he's selling for you?"

"Of course. But he doesn't leave it in a lockbox for other agents. He keeps it in his possession at all times."

"Would you mind asking Mr. Loughlin if he might have left his laptop unsecured in the mayor's presence?"

"You have got to be kidding!" The flare of dismay on

Reese's face warned Mike that he'd stepped into a mine-field.

Although he no longer worked for Mrs. Hightower, Mike had promised to keep the information about the mayor's affair confidential. That didn't apply if Roy was involved in a crime, but at this point he had no such evidence.

There's always a work-around. "The mayor does a lot of business with an escrow officer who owns a company in my complex. Yelena Yerchenko is a Russian national," he said carefully.

"Kind of a stretch, don't you think?" Reese stopped pacing, though.

"She's a very attractive woman," Mike said.

The CEO received this information coolly. "It's far-fetched, but I suppose she might have been on the property to get papers signed or something. Presumably Roy would trust her."

"If you like, I could look into this further."

Reese gave a tight nod. "Very well. But proceed with caution. If word gets out that we're investigating him, it could hurt me and my company. We're big enough to survive a libel suit or whatever he might throw at us. I'm not so sure about you."

No need to elaborate. Even aside from the possibility of a court judgment, Roy Hightower was a popular man among the general public and with Mike's former colleagues. The mayor had long been a staunch supporter of the police department. "I'll be careful."

They shook hands again. As Mike left, he recalled how hard he'd wished for a fresh lead in this case. Well, he'd found it.

Damn.

Chapter Thirteen

The last patient Paige felt like seeing on Friday was Sheila Obermeier, who'd come in for a consult.

"Gil refuses to go to the appointment with Dr. Rattigan!" the petite blonde announced the moment Paige entered the examining room. Sitting on a chair fully dressed, Mike's ex-wife radiated indignation. "He says it's insulting to think there might be anything wrong with him. As if it's just fine to assume the problem's entirely with me!"

Paige pummeled her rebellious emotions into a small box and set them aside. This was a patient who needed her help. Paige's own issues, which had tormented her since Tuesday, had no right to interfere.

"I believe there's an underlying issue that he hasn't discussed with you. Maybe he hasn't completely identified it in his own mind," she said.

"What kind of issue?" Sheila asked.

"That's hard to say. A skilled counselor could bring it out." Paige felt like a nag, harping on the same advice, but Sheila's marriage hung in the balance.

"I told you, he won't go. Honestly, I'm ready to give him an ultimatum. Put up or shut up." Tears darkened the woman's eyelashes. "Holidays make it worse. My mom and stepdad live in Alaska, and Gil doesn't have close family, either. Mike might have been gone a lot, but he had a great family. Like this weekend, for the Fourth of July, they always got together and it felt so warm and wonderful. If I had kids, we could celebrate on our own, but just me and Gil—it's not very festive." She swallowed.

"That must be tough." Having grown up with a thundering horde of relatives, Paige had enjoyed spending quiet holidays with Aunt Bree and a few friends. Now that Bree was gone, though, that had changed.

Is this what my baby has to look forward to? Holidays spent wishing he had a bunch of people to love him?

She tore her attention back to Sheila, who was saying, "You're his housemate, right? I'll bet they invited you to the party this weekend. They'll probably welcome you like family."

"I've only met them briefly," Paige said, uncomfortable with the personal turn of the conversation.

"You said you live at the beach. Are they coming to your place?"

"No, my house is too small. They're just borrowing my refrigerator."

"But they're meeting at the beach here in Safe Harbor!" Sheila brightened. "Gil and I were thinking of having a picnic. Maybe we'll run into them."

Oh, no. Paige could have kicked herself for revealing the location of the get-together. Nothing she could do about that now, though. "I suggest you avoid mentioning Dr. Rattigan for now. Instead, wait for a quiet moment and see if you can get your husband to discuss why he's so reluctant to get tested."

"I just need to apply the right kind of pressure." Sheila sniffled. "I always feel better after I talk to you."

Paige wasn't sure she'd helped. She might even have made things worse, and created an awkward situation for the Aarons, she mused as she shook hands before escorting the patient out.

At least she had something else to worry about than how she was going to tell Mike about her pregnancy.

"ME GO SWIMMING!" CRIED the three-year-old girl, and pelted across the beach past a large umbrella and a sand castle, heading for the waves.

"Graciela, wait!" Her dad, his black hair close-cropped as befitted a marine, raced to swoop her up.

"I can't turn my back on her for a minute. Thank goodness Sam's home from overseas," said her mother, Lourdes, one of Mike's stepsisters. The cheerful brunette leaned back in her woven beach chair, keeping a close eye on her fifteen-month-old son as he rolled in the sand.

Seated on a beach towel, Paige hugged her knees, enjoying the controlled chaos of a family gathering. The elder Aarons, Nina and Joe, had arrived early to stake out a prime spot for their blue-and-white canopy and canvas chairs. Paige's refrigerator and kitchen had filled up with food and ice, while extra picnic supplies weighed down her table. Not that she minded.

Nearly noon, and there'd been no sign of Sheila. All morning, Paige had tried to convince herself that the woman wouldn't be brassy enough to crash her ex-husband's family gathering. Aside from that, Gil was certain to veto the idea.

Here came a welcome distraction: Mike, carting a large wicker basket under his mother's supervision, while his brother toted a six-pack of soda and a fresh bag of ice to refill the cooler. Bright midday sunshine washed across Mike's half-naked body, caressing his sculpted torso above minuscule red trunks and reminding her of what she'd been missing all week.

Since Tuesday, she hadn't felt like making love. With their tight schedules, she'd had a ready excuse, but Mike had looked hurt when she ducked his invitations. To a guy, a few days must seem like an eternity.

Whatever Paige was going to say, she'd better get it out soon before he noticed the gradual change in her figure. Today, she'd worn shorts and a T-shirt as a precaution.

"Are we ready to eat? I'm starving!" Erica announced from the far side of the canopy, where she'd been talking intently with Renée Green, Lock's birth mother.

At five months along, the mother-to-be was blooming—and wisely staying out of the sun. An increase in pigmentation could cause a darkening of the face known as the mask of pregnancy or, technically, chloasma. Also, Erica's light coloring made her vulnerable to burning and skin cancer. *Not as much as being a redhead,* Paige reflected, and reached for her tube of sunscreen to apply another round.

"Erica, come eat. Lourdes, bring the little ones. We've got chips and dips and sandwiches, all nice and fresh, thanks to Paige's fridge." Nina Aaron bathed Paige in a smile. "You've been such a help!"

"I've hardly done anything, but thanks," Paige responded, embarrassed. Mike's mother had showered her with warmth all day, no doubt based on the belief that she and Mike were an item. While that wasn't entirely wrong, Paige didn't want to encourage expectations considering that things were due to come crashing to earth any day now.

Mike dropped down beside her. "Let me do that." Sliding the slippery tube from her grasp, he squeezed a dollop into his palm.

She felt half a dozen pairs of interested eyes fix on them. "I can manage."

"You can't reach your back. I've heard people can burn right through T-shirts." Without warning, he tugged hers up to bare her waist and back. "See? About to turn pink any minute." Strong fingers smoothed the cream along her spine and around the band of her bra.

A lovely tingle ran from his fingertips down her spine. Paige leaned forward onto liquid knees, her breasts heavy with longing for him to reach around and stroke them.

She felt herself blushing. For heaven's sake, how could she think about such things in front of his whole family?

Everyone had redirected their attention to the food, but they couldn't have missed the way he'd lifted her shirt high enough to expose the back of her bra. While that was no big deal on a beach where women trailed about in crocheted bikinis the size of spiderwebs, it removed any pretense that they were merely housemates.

As soon as she could, she eased her shirt down. "Mike! People are watching."

He rocked back on his heels. "What's eating you?"

"I just don't want to give your family the wrong idea."

"What idea is that?" he asked.

Did they have to discuss this within earshot of the others? Although the murmur of waves provided a partial sound screen, it was hardly foolproof. "I mean, that there's anything serious."

"I assure you, no one's planning to hire a catering hall anytime soon," he told her sharply. "Are you trying to get back at me?"

"What?"

Even though he kept his voice low, there was no mistaking the note of anger. "There's been a distinct chill since you learned I'm a sperm donor. Is this your way of punishing me?"

"For what?"

"Not wanting to have kids."

"Absolutely not." The idea astonished her. "I would never try to manipulate..." She broke off abruptly.

Toward them across the sand trekked Sheila in a hot-pink swimsuit that revealed a wealth of curves and a flat stomach flashing a jeweled navel ring. Behind her, a pudgy Gil halted in his tracks, dropping the chairs and beach bag he'd been carrying. "You didn't tell me your ex-husband would be here!"

Mike returned the man's glare. "What the hell is this?"

"Hey! How great to see everybody!" Sheila crowed. "Nina! Lourdes! Where's Marianne?"

"Here." Mike's sister, drenched from bodysurfing, hiked toward them from the waterline. "Sheila, it's nice to see you. What, uh...?"

Ignoring the unfinished question, Sheila went on greeting everyone as if they were her best friends in the world. Gil stood rooted to the spot, clearly torn between outrage and embarrassment.

Sheila must have come here to punish her husband for his lack of cooperation, Paige thought. That was the kind of passive-aggressive behavior Mike had grown accustomed to during his marriage, and here it was, right under their noses. Did the woman truly believe that putting her husband into such an uncomfortable position would make him change his mind about getting tested?

Moreover, Gil's body language spoke volumes. Folded arms, hips angled away, and agitated glances at Mike gave Paige a strong clue about the man's inner turmoil. While Gil had good reason to be uncomfortable around the man whose wife he'd stolen, his self-conscious movements told an additional story. Unless she missed her guess, Mike's blatant masculinity threatened the guy. Overweight and out of shape, Gil looked like a chubby wolf forced to confront the alpha male in a pack.

No wonder he shrank from medical testing that might reveal a fertility problem. What to Paige seemed purely a medical matter added to Gil's feelings of falling short in comparison to Sheila's former husband. Today's contrast, unmistakable in their swimsuits, could only heighten the problem. If Sheila had meant to goad her husband into cooperating, she'd probably achieved the opposite effect by making him even more insecure.

Paige tuned back into the conversation. After breezily acknowledging Lock's introduction to his new wife, Sheila was responding to a question from Marianne. "Well, okay, I did spring a teensy-weensy surprise on my husband, but a little bird told me you'd all be here."

Paige realized her talkative patient was about to make things much worse with Mike. If only she could head this off, give Sheila a signal or something…but aside from throwing sand in the woman's face, that didn't seem possible.

So Paige sat there cringing as Mike's ex-wife announced in shrill tones, "It seemed too good to be true when Dr. Brennan mentioned yesterday that you'd all be here today. I've missed you terribly!"

Mike turned to Paige in astonishment. "You invited her?"

"It slipped out." She bit down on any further words rather than reveal privileged information.

Nina Aaron, who'd greeted her former daughter-in-law warily, stepped into the breach. "Dr. Brennan, you said? You must be one of Paige's patients."

Silently, Paige thanked Mike's mother. There was no prohibition on someone else guessing the truth, especially when Sheila herself had supplied the hint.

Mike's expression turned sheepish. Close to Paige's ear, he said, "*That's* what's been bothering you? Sorry I jumped to conclusions. If she gave you the impression I want her here, she was lying."

Paige nodded. While she didn't mean to leave him with the mistaken idea that she'd withdrawn this week because of his ex-wife, they couldn't discuss her real reason now.

The tension broke when a dripping wet Graciela scampered up with her father in her wake. "I'm hungry! Where's lunch?" With her dark hair whipping in the breeze and her eyes as round as a doll's, the little girl was adorable.

Paige glanced at Gil. His harshness melted, and in that instant she saw a flash of tenderness. Averting his gaze quickly, he stiffened his shoulders.

The man really did want children. Sheila needed to quit pushing his buttons and let him know that he had nothing to fear.

While Sam took his daughter to the picnic basket, the Aaron family members politely brought Sheila up to date on their activities. No one invited her to sit down and eat with them, however.

Gil remained apart, arms folded. While it wasn't Paige's job to save their relationship nor had anyone appointed her protector of the Aarons, she did feel bad about contributing to the problem. Most important, there was something Sheila needed to hear.

Rising, she commandeered the smaller woman by touching her elbow. "I don't mean to interrupt, but may I have a word?"

"Uh, okay." After a moment's hesitation, the blonde accompanied Paige closer to the roadway, at the edge of the sand. "I didn't mean to cause trouble for you, Dr. Brennan. I wanted Gil to see what it's like to have a real family gathering. You're not mad, are you?"

"This is about you, not me." Firmly, Paige forged ahead. "I'm going to give you some straight talk as your doctor. Your husband wants kids but he's insecure around Mike. Don't ask me how I know, but I do. What he needs is reassurance that you find him masculine and desirable."

Sheila's face scrunched in protest. "It's hard to find him masculine and adorable when he won't see Dr. Rattigan."

"You aren't hearing me." Paige didn't usually come down so hard on patients, especially with advice that wasn't strictly medical, but Sheila had crossed a line. She'd taken advantage of an innocent disclosure to barge into today's gathering. If Sheila could push boundaries, so could Paige. "Do you want children?"

"You know I do!"

"Then follow this prescription." Angled away from the others, Paige hoped they weren't picking up her stern demeanor. She had a feeling Mike would, though. Mr. Detective was too darn observant. "Take your husband somewhere private and apologize to him. Tell him that seeing Mike reminded you of how glad you are that you left him."

"I don't see how that will help."

"A man's ego is fragile, no matter how tough he acts. When you diminish your husband's pride, you drive him away." Inspiration hit. "Pick up a fistful of sand."

"What?" Sheila blinked.

"Just do it."

Dubiously, the woman scooped a handful of sand.

"Now squeeze!" Paige ordered.

With an uncertain air, Sheila obeyed. A trickle of sand ran out both sides of her fist.

"Harder!"

More sand fell to the beach.

"Open your hand." Paige indicated the thin wedge of remaining sand. "Not much left, is there?"

Sheila shook her head.

"Pick up another handful." After the woman complied, Paige said, "Hold your hand open. What happens to the sand?"

"Nothing." Sheila sounded puzzled.

"That's right. Love is like that. The harder you squeeze, the faster it runs out on you. When you hold it gently, it stays," Paige told her. "Now go home and hold Gil in the palm of your hand, and stop squeezing him out."

When Sheila didn't react, Paige feared her words had been wasted. Then the woman took a deep breath. "You really think he feels threatened?"

"Yes."

Dropping the sand, she brushed off her palm. "You're the doctor. I'll give it a try."

Paige remained in place as Sheila trudged back to the Aarons. She watched the woman take her leave in a friendly manner, and then help Gil collect their gear. Off they went.

Across the sand, Nina Aaron circled her thumb and forefinger at Paige, giving her the "okay" sign of approval. As for Mike, he stared at her in amazement. Then cut over to Paige, meeting her halfway back to the group.

"That was incredible." He looped an arm around her waist. "What did you say to her?"

"Doctor-patient privilege," she replied lightly.

"Whatever you did, I wish I'd had that secret years ago. Nobody's ever been able to make Sheila shut up and behave."

Paige started to laugh. Quickly, she checked on Sheila's whereabouts, and was glad to see her and Gil disappearing toward the beach parking lot. "I didn't think of it in those terms."

When they reached the group, Paige found herself surrounded. "That was incredible. What did you do?" Marianne asked, sounding just like her brother.

"Doctor-patient privilege," Mike responded, saving her the need to reply.

"Do you treat men?" his father asked. "Because if you're that much of a miracle worker in the clinic, I'm switching doctors."

"Until men can get pregnant, I'm afraid not." But she relished the lighthearted compliment. "Now, how about a sandwich?"

With Sheila's departure, a new spirit of enthusiasm animated the group. Laughter echoed, and Paige basked in the sense of acceptance. Oddly, she realized she'd never been this at ease with her own family, perhaps because they'd cast her in the outgrown, chafing role of the youngest.

Along with a few of the Aarons and some other beachgoers, Paige and Mike started a game of volleyball. For the first few exchanges, Mike and Lock—on opposite sides of the net—pounded each other hard. Then a couple of children joined in, and everyone had to be careful not to hurt or scare them. Mike dropped his sibling rivalry to coach a boy of about ten, showing him how to serve the ball and cheering when it arced over the net.

He was good at this, a natural father. But Paige knew better than to mention that touchy subject.

After the game, Lock took Erica home for a nap and Lourdes and Sam bundled up their two exhausted children. "We'd love to stay for the fireworks, but that'll have to wait till they're older," Lourdes said wistfully.

In the past, Paige had learned, the family often met at

a park inland or at the Aarons' home. So there might not be fireworks next year, although they could come to this public beach even if she weren't part of the picture. Still, having the use of her kitchen to store things had been an obvious plus.

Why was she worrying about this? She'd known all along that what she and Mike had couldn't last. But no one else knew it yet.

Paige longed to hold on to this day forever. When Mike applied more sunscreen, tracing her nose with his thumb and brushing a kiss across her mouth, Paige didn't fuss. Next year, where would she be? Next year, who would Mike bring to the picnic? Her heart clenched at the thought of him with someone else.

As the afternoon stretched into evening, more family members arrived, including a foster brother, Denzel, with a new girlfriend, and another foster sister, Fatima, with her husband and baby. People took walks to the harbor, and others played a round of Monopoly on an iPad. Twilight fell, and then darkness.

From a barge towed offshore, fireworks lit the sky. Like fairy lights from another world, red, white and blue burst across the night sky. As the breeze cooled, Paige pulled on a jacket and rested in Mike's arms, lying back to gaze up at the starry brilliance.

His warmth flowed around her, and she got lost in the musky scent of sun-touched skin and masculine longing. The joy of the day outshone the questions that kept trying to surface until they finally gave up the battle. For now.

Overhead, fountains of color gushed and snapped, transforming the world. No matter what happened tomorrow, this moment would remain burned into Paige's memory with all its splendor and happiness.

In a little while, she and Mike would go home together. Selfishly, she was going to enjoy him one more time.

Then she could no longer delay telling him the truth. Or as much of it as she dared.

Chapter Fourteen

Tonight, making love with Paige surpassed anything Mike had experienced before. She gripped him with renewed fervor, and he felt himself opening up to her in a new way. Needing her, merging with her, trusting her.

In the tiny rear courtyard, they'd rinsed off the sand, shivering in the cold water from the hose, then adjourned to the bathroom to strip off their swimsuits and plunge into the heat of the shower. The droplets had steamed off their bodies as they stroked each other.

Now, in her bed, he hardly knew where he ended and she began. Nor did it matter. He admired her, belonged with her and…

A great shuddering climax wiped away thought. Sensations rocketed through him fiercer and brighter than fireworks. He cried out, and heard Paige moan deliriously as she clutched him.

He didn't want to release her. Only the slow fading of ecstasy allowed him finally to relax beside the woman he…

Loved.

Where was the terror? The instinctive withdrawal? How strange to recall that, all week, he'd attributed her preoccupation to some sort of trick. She hadn't been pushing him away. She'd just been trying to balance her feelings for him with her care, as a doctor, for his ex-wife.

The way she'd handled Sheila had been masterful. Seeing his new lady vanquish the old dragon had symbolically cleared the field, Mike supposed, and smiled at the image.

"That was unforgettable," he said.

"This whole day was unforgettable." Page released a sigh.

"My family adores you." No exaggeration. As they were taking down the canopy this evening, Mike's father had advised him quietly, "Don't let this one get away."

"I feel the same way about them."

The plaintive note in her voice struck him. "You make it sound as if you're never going to see them again."

"I told you about Nora's offer. That I have to decide whether to buy into the practice or relocate to be near my family."

He didn't recall that last part. It made no sense. "You weren't sure about taking on such a big financial commitment, but I can't believe you'd consider for one minute moving back to Texas. What's going on, Paige?"

An uneasy sensation twisted inside him as, in the glow of the bedside lamp, he studied her face. The winged eyebrows, the expressive mouth, the sweet sprinkling of freckles across her cheeks. He'd never felt this close to anyone before. Had his emotions blinded him? He'd certainly misjudged Sheila when he fell for her, but their courtship had never been like this. Never this open or honest.

At least, he assumed they were both being honest. Yet she hadn't told him she was considering moving away.

Paige sat up, stretching her legs. "I don't know any easy way to say this, so here goes. I'm pregnant."

The last word echoed inside Mike like the vibrations of a huge gong. Pregnant. Starts with a *p,* ends with a baby. Oh, hell. He didn't see how this could have happened. "I'm sorry. I was careful to use protection."

"What?" She gave a start. "Oh, no. It's not your...I mean...I was pregnant before you moved in. I'm two months along."

"There's some other guy you never told me about?" Mike felt sucker punched. How could she have withheld so much information from him? "Here I believed you were being up front with me all along."

He shook his head in disgust, almost as much with himself as with her. He'd begun to hope that their growing intimacy meant she might be reconsidering her desire to have children. That would have meant a lot. Instead, she'd been deceiving him their entire time together.

Paige wrapped her arms around her chest. "Our relationship was only supposed to be for the summer. You don't want kids, and I wouldn't expect a guy to raise someone else's child."

"So you figured no harm, no foul?" That hurt. But tempted as he was to lash out, Mike had to acknowledge a certain cosmic irony. If anyone had asked him at the start how he saw this affair ending, he'd have agreed with her assessment, more or less.

"Something like that."

She hadn't deliberately tricked him, Mike conceded. But he felt blindsided, and she was still holding out. "What about this guy?"

"What guy? Oh." In the dim light, her pupils widened.

"Like, the father." He made no attempt to hide his sarcasm.

"Well, um."

What was the big deal? Mike took a guess. "He's married."

"No!"

Frustrated, he ran a hand through his hair. "It's like I don't know you at all. You've been lying to me for weeks and now…"

"I have not!"

"Lying by omission," he countered. "And you're still playing games." He wanted the truth about this other man, the one she'd been sleeping with only a few weeks before she got together with him.

"This is complicated." Paige pulled the quilt to her chin. Then doubled up and slid down until it covered her face.

For a guy who prided himself on his insights, Mike was having a hard time putting the clues together. That might be because he wasn't examining them logically.

His mind sorted over the past few weeks and landed squarely on Tuesday. Her reaction to learning he was a sperm donor had been out of proportion. And he recalled her question about when he'd started, as if that made any difference.

April. The month that comes before May.

And sometime in there, Paige had conceived a child.

Once, while chasing a suspect, Mike had leaped a vine-draped fence onto what he assumed was level ground, only to hit a steep downward slope and have his feet shoot out from under him. He got the same sensation now. Big thud, uncontrolled fall.

"You had artificial insemination." Pressure built at the base of his throat. "It's mine. That's what you're not telling me?"

The covers nodded.

"And you figured this out Tuesday." Must have been almost as big a shock to her as it was to him.

Paige propelled herself into view. "Mike, I had no intention of putting you in this position."

"You're pregnant with my baby." Although they'd already covered that point, he struggled to grasp the reality.

"I could run a DNA test." She spoke apologetically. "But I reviewed the descriptions of all the sperm donors and compared them to the one I chose, and no one else comes close. You're firing on all cylinders, so to speak."

That sounded convincing. As a detective, he'd go for the DNA test if she were making demands, but apparently she wasn't.

Walk away. She has no right to stop you. That was his gut instinct shouting, loud and clear. Yet, unbidden, a picture unscrolled of Lourdes's little girl running across the sand, dark hair bouncing, face bright with happiness. Like it or not, Mike was going to be a father. Damn, he couldn't begin to sort this out.

"You thought it was fair to conceive a kid with no father involved?" He hadn't meant to speak harshly, but the more he thought about it, the more selfish the idea struck him.

"I'd given up on meeting the right guy." Paige choked a little, and coughed. "Rotten timing."

"I'd have been the wrong guy, by definition."

"Yeah. I probably wouldn't have gone to bed with you if I'd been looking for the father type." She smiled wanly. "Strange but true."

"Now I get to be a father whether I like it or not."

"Oh, come on!" Her sharp tone signaled that she was done taking the blame. "What did you think was going to happen when you became a sperm donor? That the only women who'd use your studly services would be married ladies with infertile husbands?"

"I didn't… Actually, yes."

"You were wrong."

"I see that."

Despite the defiant lift of her chin, tears formed a sheen in her eyes. "You can move out now if you want. Or stay till September. I hope your family won't hold this against me."

"Are you kidding? They'll hold it against *me*." He had no intention of telling them—but there'd be no way to keep it a secret once her pregnancy began to show. After all, she was Erica's doctor.

As well as Sheila's. Oh, crap.

And in the end, there was going to be a child. Whether it grew up in California or Texas, whether he claimed it or not, he'd never be able to forget that Paige was raising his son or daughter.

Going through it alone. Or not. Plenty of guys would be glad to step in. Men raised other men's children all the time, and Paige was a damn attractive woman.

"I can't make a decision right now." Mike swung out of bed. "What a mess."

"I didn't do this on purpose, and I'm not asking you to decide anything," she reminded him. "Did you have to be such a desirable sperm donor?"

"It's all my fault?"

"That was a joke."

Mike's brother had once accused him of having a capricious sense of humor. Well, it had deserted him now. "Not in a funny mood." He grabbed his damp towel off the carpet, where he'd dropped it when they careered into the bedroom.

Her arms circling her raised knees, Paige resembled an Irish angel haloed in lamplight. "I'll miss you."

Mike stalked out without responding. Because if he did, he'd have to admit he was going to miss her, too. And that hurt like hell.

ON SUNDAY MORNING, BENEATH a typically gray sky that would yield to brilliant blue by midday, Paige sat on the patio drinking tea and wishing Mike were beside her instead of hidden behind his closed door. Across the street, Willy and the new guy at the halfway house shuffled by, casting irritated glances in Paige's direction as if her presence interfered with their activities. If so, good, because even with her watching they kept peering into the cars parked along the curb.

It was comforting to know Mike was inside. And after he left? Well, with luck, these particular guys might be gone, as well. They weren't permanent residents, after all.

I might not be here then, either.

Paige's stomach churned. The orderly future she'd planned had come crashing in on her. Go to Texas? Stay in Safe Harbor alone?

She'd missed waking up with Mike this morning. Missed him with a deep, powerful ache that refused to go away. While he'd given no indication that he planned to move out immediately, it appeared their affair was at an end.

How did they go on from here until summer's end? Acting civil but keeping apart? If only they could find their way back to each other, even for a while. But after that...

Her eyes burned. Stupid, stupid heart. Why did it have to love a man she couldn't have? She'd known they weren't compatible, but she'd fooled herself into believing it was safe to indulge for a few months.

As for last night, he'd reacted about the way she'd expected. He hadn't stooped to groundless accusations, but he'd taken no interest in the baby, either.

Paige's hand dropped to her abdomen as she recalled his words. *You thought it was fair to conceive a kid with no father involved?* He had a point. But the alternative was no child at all. And she loved this one with a ferocity that burned right through the cloud cover to rival the sun hidden overhead.

Now she had to put her baby's best interests first. And much as it hurt to think of leaving this beloved place, her child deserved more than a single mom raising it alone.

Taking out her cell phone, Paige wondered which of her siblings to call. Now that the moment had arrived to inform them of her pregnancy, she realized this was going to be a challenge.

Six months ago, she'd informed her oldest sister Juno of Aunt Bree's death and invited her to the memorial service. After asking a few pointed questions, Juno had turned up her nose on learning that instead of a funeral, Bree had requested an informal service on the beach at which Paige and a few longtime friends would give testimony to her life and read from inspirational texts. As for the plan to scatter Bree's ashes at sea rather than bury them in a cemetery, that had apparently been the last straw.

"I'm sorry she's dead. I know how close you were," Paige's older sister had told her briskly. "But my family needs me here."

Their middle sister, Maeve, had claimed she wasn't feeling well enough to travel. To Paige's concerned inquiry, she'd responded with vague generalities. Maeve had always been something of a hypochondriac, dosing herself with vitamin concoctions and claiming that, as a nurse, she knew best.

The only member of the Brennan clan to make the trip had been the middle brother, Dermot, an obstetrician in Austin who'd planned to attend a medical conference in Los Angeles the following week. He'd delivered a few words about what a colorful person Bree had been in their otherwise conservative family, and added that he had no doubt she and their dad had already resumed their political debates in the next life. Regardless of the fact that flying west more or less fit into his schedule, Paige had appreciated his participation.

They'd exchanged a few emails since then, a mix of family news, jokes and inspirational quotes. She'd better phone now, before she lost her nerve, and besides, she went on call at the hospital soon. It was two hours later in Texas, so her brother should be home from church.

Paige pressed the number in her cell. The familiar nasal voice that answered belonged to his wife, Billy Lee. After exchanging pleasantries, Paige asked to speak to her brother.

"He'll be glad to hear from you," Billy Lee said cheerily. "I'll just go grab him." In the background, Paige heard the babble of childish voices. She'd lost count of how many grandchildren Dermot and Billy Lee's five kids had produced, but they obviously enjoyed visiting the grandparents.

An explosion of giggling leaped across the roughly fifteen hundred miles between Austin and Safe Harbor, right into her ear. It reminded her how much Baby Bree or Brian would enjoy being surrounded by cousins.

"Paige!" Her brother's friendly but puzzled voice came over the phone. "It's good to hear from you."

No sense beating around the bush. "I'm—" A lump

clogged Paige's throat. "I'm thinking of moving back to Texas. Wanted to sound you out about medical practices."

"Really? That's great." A brief pause. "Mind if I ask why? I'm thrilled, but I had the impression you were settled out there."

Let's get this over with. "I'm pregnant." To head off the obvious questions, she added, "Intentionally. I used a donor." If anyone in the family would understand, surely it was a fellow obstetrician.

"I see." She pictured Dermot as he'd looked at the funeral: a rangy six-plus footer, his once-bright russet hair turning gray. "Um, congratulations. We'll be glad to have you. Don't forget you'll need a Texas medical license. That can take a few months."

"I know." She'd already checked the information on the internet.

"You're serious about this? Coming back here, I mean."

"I'm seriously considering it."

"We might very well have room for you in our practice. I'm sure Gray would agree." That was his longtime medical partner. "We've got more patients than we can handle."

"Terrific!" This might work out better than she'd hoped, Paige thought, trying to ignore the tightening in her gut. Considering that she'd dropped a big surprise on her brother, he was responding with as much enthusiasm as she could expect. "If things work out for me to join you, I'll want to buy into the practice. This may be premature, but I'm mentioning it so you and Gray can consider it now."

"You mean, join as an equal partner?"

"That's the idea." It seemed a good idea for her future stability. Also, her brother was in his early fifties. While retirement was still more than a decade away, at some point he and Gray would want to hand over the reins to a younger generation.

He cleared his throat. "That might be something to consider later. Initially, let's talk about you joining as an employee. Once the baby comes, you'll only want to work part-time anyway."

"Perhaps for a few months, but I plan to return full-time."

"Sweetie, take it from me. Once you hold that baby in your arms, you'll be astonished how much you change."

A flare of resentment nearly overwhelmed Paige's usually even temper. Of course she knew that motherhood would affect her, but if she chose to invest her money and make a commitment, she was experienced and adult enough to own that decision.

Nearby, the front door opened. Her body tingled as Mike strolled out, jeans hugging his muscular legs and a sky-blue polo shirt emphasizing his tanned throat and neck. After a nod of greeting, he settled into a lounge chair near Paige and opened his laptop on his knees.

"We'll have to discuss this further, Dermot," she said. "As I said, I'm not ready to…"

"Have you spoken to your sisters?"

"Not yet." Paige supposed she'd have to. No use trying to keep her pregnancy confidential now. Her brother would tell Billy Lee, and she'd hit the dial button so fast she'd sprain her finger.

"Give them a call. You could use some mature advice at a time like this," Dermot said.

And you could use a good kick in the big-brother syndrome. "I'll consider what we discussed."

"Gray and I would like to have a female on staff. The patients would love it. Paige, I'm doing you a favor by not letting you rush into something. Things are going to be very different once the baby comes."

"We'll talk again, bro."

"You bet, kiddo."

After ending the call, Paige fought down the temptation to throw her phone across the patio. That would be childish, and it might damage the device. Instead, she stomped her feet against the bricks in a rapid drumbeat, before reflecting that that was pretty immature, too. But less expensive.

Looking up from his work, Mike regarded her in amusement. "One of your brothers?"

"He called me 'sweetie' and 'kiddo'! He wants me to join his practice as an employee and work part-time after I give birth." Paige's fists pummeled the air. "Rat fink! Sexist twit!"

"You cuss like a girl."

"Don't you start!" she roared.

Mike's chuckle faded into pensiveness. "You're really planning to move to Texas?"

"Maybe. I failed to consider how annoying families can be." Wistfully, she added, "Not yours."

"They've been known to rub me the wrong way."

Her irritation subsiding, Paige gazed fondly at the man who'd made heart-stopping love to her last night. "I like having you around to yell at."

Regret shadowed his blue-gray eyes. "Me, too. Paige, I'm sorry this isn't working out."

His quiet resignation hurt more than any accusing words. "Me, too." Her phone buzzed. "Probably one of my sisters. That was quick." She'd guessed wrong, she discovered from the display. "It's the hospital. Gotta go help perform a few miracles."

"Returning to Texas—you won't be happy there. I

mean, you've got this great home, and your friends at the hospital."

"It's just one option on my plate." She waited, hoping he would add that she had him, too, at least for now.

"See you later, Doc," Mike said, and returned to his computer.

More hurt than she'd expected, Paige got to her feet. Her alternative of moving to Texas was becoming less appealing by the minute. But staying here without Mike wasn't an option she relished, either.

Well, she was in charge of her life, and one way or the other, she planned to make the best of things.

Chapter Fifteen

Mike couldn't even go to the bathroom without the latest copy of *Today's Baby* staring at him from the magazine rack. Did every edition have to feature an adorable tyke beaming from the cover? Just once, they ought to show an unshaven, bleary-eyed father with a soiled receiving blanket slung over his shoulder.

Flipping the thing open, he scowled at the articles on decorating a nursery and ads for baby furniture. It didn't seem right that he'd moved out of one house in part to escape the pending arrival of his nephew, only to learn that his new, comfortable bedroom was to be transformed into yet another baby haven.

Unless Paige moved to Texas. He hoped she'd reconsider after the way her brother had reduced her to a fury. Still, that wouldn't do Mike any good.

As he stuffed the magazine into its rack, a funny thing happened to his peripheral vision. The almond-eyed tot on the cover transformed, for a flash, into a cocky little boy with red hair and freckles.

His kid. And Paige's.

Give me a break!

Back to work. On the patio, Mike ignored the increasing numbers of pedestrians flip-flopping their way to the beach. Holiday weekend, emerging sunshine, and here he sat knocking his brains out trying to get a break in the Kendall prototype theft. If it didn't happen soon, Reese would have no choice but to call in the feds and let them run amok through his company. To Mike, that meant failure. *His* failure to his most important client.

He'd been trying since Thursday to get hold of Doug Loughlin, but the engineer had left early for the holiday weekend and apparently wasn't answering his calls. Or maybe the guy had something to hide.

An alert popped up on the screen. Mike had registered for alerts on key figures in case any of them hit the internet, which Roy Hightower had just done.

Mike clicked a link that connected him to *On the Prowl in OC*, an Orange County video news program hosted by Ian Martin, a former international reporter who'd married Safe Harbor Medical's public relations director a couple of years ago and settled here to write books on medical and social issues. His latest was entitled *Unexpecting: The Surprising Impact of Modern Fertility Treatments.* But while his program usually dealt with medical issues, he'd branched out into California politics, as well. Mike watched occasionally to keep tabs on developments that might affect his company.

When he started the video, Mike recognized the setting immediately: a custom pool overlooking a spectacular view of the harbor. He'd seen that same view when he'd met with Gemma Hightower at her home.

Seated beside her husband, she wore a plastic smile and a flowing blue pantsuit with an American flag pinned to the collar, coordinated with Roy's blue jacket, red pinstriped shirt and white pants. At right angles to them, the show's lean, blond host faced the camera with practiced ease.

"Safe Harbor Mayor Roy Hightower has just announced his candidacy for the state assembly in next year's elections. His wife, Gemma, is serving as campaign manager. Mayor, why are you making the announcement so early?"

Someone must have applied makeup to the mayor's jowly face, because no shine broke through the smooth finish, Mike noted. Every aspect of this announcement had been choreographed.

"My wife encouraged me to throw my hat in the ring early to kick off the fundraising and let any potential opponents know they're up against the front-runner." Behind the smile that Roy cast at Gemma, Mike caught a hint of appeal. "I rely on my wife above everything. We will celebrate our thirtieth anniversary this fall. I'm prouder of that than of all my accomplishments in business and city government."

To Mike, the comment explained a lot. Knowing her husband's political ambitions, Gemma Hightower had most likely confronted him about his cheating and insisted on this move. Increased media attention plus the threat of an ugly divorce torpedoing his chances must have forced him to end the affair, or at any rate put it on hold. With one stroke, Gemma had bested her rival and cemented her own position as vital to her husband's future.

Mike missed whatever Roy said next. Then the camera pulled back to reveal a fourth participant in the interview, and he nearly stopped breathing.

"I'm here to let everyone know I support Mayor Hightower as our future assemblyman," said the familiar voice of Safe Harbor Police Chief Jon Walters. With his cropped hair and military bearing, the man commanded instant respect. And deserved it.

His support carried a lot of weight. When the day came

for Mike to run for county sheriff, he'd intended to ask for the chief's endorsement.

Maybe it was a good thing that he hadn't been able to pin any wrongdoing on Roy. Doing so now would publicly embarrass Chief Walters.

Still, Mike's first obligation was to his client. He watched the rest of the interview, only half listening to the discussion of issues facing the state legislature. Then he put in yet another call to Doug Loughlin's number.

BY LATE AFTERNOON, WHEN Paige finally got a break from delivering babies, she still hadn't heard from her sisters. Were they angry with her for some reason, or just too tied up today to react to the news?

Might as well get this over with. She wanted to clear the air before she decided whether to live near them.

Resting on a couch in the doctors' lounge, Paige put in a call to Juno. It would have been easier to start with Maeve, since, as the eldest, Juno tended to be bossy. But if Paige couldn't face the queen bee, she certainly wasn't strong enough to take on the entire clan.

By the fifth ring, she was about to give up when her sister's softly accented voice said, "Paige? I've been wondering when we'd hear from you."

"I'm on call at the hospital today," she answered, avoiding any trace of apology. No sense starting off in an inferior position. "You've heard from Billy Lee, I gather."

"She was all too happy to get the jump on me." In the background, a TV set blared. "Just a minute. Aldo's watching baseball. I'll take the phone into the kitchen."

"I didn't mean to interrupt."

"That's no problem. Just a silly old ball game. Hold on a sec. I trip over my feet if I talk while I'm moving."

Listening to background rustling, Paige could picture

her sister walking through the sprawling ranch-style house where she and her husband, Aldo, had raised three children and where the family held Christmas gatherings. Paige had missed the last one. So soon after Bree's death, she'd have been a drag on everyone else's holiday spirit.

"You still there, honey?" Juno asked.

"Still here." Paige glanced up as Jared Sellers's dark head poked into the lounge. The neonatologist brightened when he spotted her, then noticed she was on the phone and withdrew.

"When's your little darling due?" asked her sister.

"Early February." As she spoke, Paige realized she hadn't even considered the fact that she'd have to switch doctors if she moved. But things might not happen that fast, what with the need to sell her house and qualify for a Texas medical license.

"I guess I shouldn't be surprised you're doing this without a husband. That's Aunt Bree's influence," Juno said. "I don't mean to criticize."

"Okay," Paige said guardedly.

"Before we go any further, there's something I've been meaning to tell you."

Her sister had secrets? "Oh?"

"The reason we couldn't go to Aunt Bree's funeral, or whatever you call that service she had, is because Maeve was being treated for breast cancer."

Their middle sister had only said she didn't feel well, not that she was fighting for her life. "I wish she'd told me."

"You had enough on your plate," Juno said briskly. "Anyhow, Maeve's fine now. They caught it early thanks to her mammogram. She had surgery and radiation, and everything looks good."

"I'm glad to hear that," Paige said. "I'll call her."

"She'd like that," Juno agreed. "And, honey, don't let Dermot push you around. If you want to come back here and practice with some other doctor, that's just fine. Billy Lee eavesdropped on that whole conversation—you know her—and we both think he's being a sexist pig. I mean that in the nicest way."

Paige laughed. She'd missed Juno's sense of humor. "I haven't made a decision yet, but one way or the other, I'll visit you all as soon as I can arrange it."

"If you don't, Aldo and I are coming out there to California. My little sister is having a baby, and I do not intend to miss this."

"I'd love to see you both." Paige wound up the conversation quickly, and dialed Maeve's number. To her relief, her other sister sounded robust and energetic.

"I'm doing great," Maeve confirmed. "Sorry I didn't tell you in December but I'm not the type to throw a pity party."

"That's a lot to go through," Paige pointed out.

"Darling, I'm a nurse. I've seen it all." Maeve's remark reminded Paige that her sister was in her midforties. Hard to believe. "And June Bug—" her pet name for Juno "—swamped my kitchen with casseroles and pies. She gave me all the mothering I could've asked for. Maybe more."

They chatted for awhile longer about her husband and four kids, including a married daughter with a toddler. After the call ended, nostalgia and longing swept over Paige. Even though common sense warned that the euphoria of a reunion would quickly wear off, she couldn't wait to see her sisters again.

In the doorway, Jared reappeared. "Listen, I'm on my way out, but I had to let you know the good news. Lori took a pregnancy test and it's positive."

"That's wonderful!" Paige decided to hold off on sharing the news of her own pregnancy. "Congratulations, Dad."

"We're over the moon. And it's another credit for you in the contest."

"As if that mattered!"

"It puts you in third position, right after Owen and Mark," the father-to-be said cheerfully. "In any case, we're glad you'll be delivering her. Lori feels comfortable with you."

"I'll be honored." Only after Jared vanished did it strike Paige that she might be gone by then.

Erica was scheduled to deliver in November, the contest climaxed in December, and now Lori was expecting a baby next spring. How could Paige bear to miss those events?

She lurched to her feet. Time to check on her patients in labor. Her decision would have to wait.

ON THE COMPUTER SCREEN, Mike watched the engineer's thin face crease with outrage. Home from a camping trip, Doug Loughlin had returned his call a few minutes ago via Skype and immediately made a damning connection. Unless there were holes in his story, it was likely to derail Roy's political career…and indirectly, Mike's.

"Of all the people I wouldn't have suspected, Mayor Hightower is near the top of the list." Behind the man, the camera showed his home office bristling with electronic equipment. "I feel like flying out to California and strangling him. He played me for a fool."

"You're certain of this?" Although he'd heard the account once, Mike wasn't satisfied. With so much at stake, he'd better review the details. "Walk me through it again."

"No problem." The engineer plunged ahead. "Like I

said, I didn't think twice about leaving him alone in the house while he staged it for buyers. Frankly, I was impressed with his initiative. My wife had gone to Phoenix to look for a new house. It seemed like a big favor that he was willing to pack away some of the stuff and rearrange things a little."

"You're certain about the laptop?"

"In retrospect, I was an idiot," Doug grumbled, clenching his hands atop his cluttered desk. "It was defragging and I needed to run errands, so I left it on. Of course, it finished before I got back, so it was just sitting there, unguarded."

By itself, Roy's being alone with the laptop proved nothing. "And you clearly remember…"

"When I came in, like I told you, he was in my office. He pointed my attention out the window, yammering about how I needed to get the bushes trimmed. Later I found a message on the screen about failing to disconnect a device properly. The kind of warning you get if you pull out a flash drive in a hurry."

"But you thought nothing of it?"

"Obviously, I should have. But after I walked him to the door, it must have been ten or fifteen minutes before I sat down to work. When I saw the warning, I didn't associate it with Roy's being in the room. I'd copied a file earlier and I figured I'd made the mistake myself. I do tend to get distracted."

"I understand." Around Mike, the early-evening light etched deep shadows onto the brick patio.

"What happens now?"

"I'll take this to Reese tomorrow," Mike said. "After that, it's up to him."

"The man stole our prototype!" Doug fumed. "He cost

us a bundle. Not to mention betraying our trust. He deserves to be marched away in handcuffs."

Probably true, although more investigation would be needed. If Doug himself had committed the theft, he had reason to lie about the mayor. But Mike's instincts sided with the engineer. He just wished that Roy Hightower's downfall wasn't likely to create a problem for Chief Walters.

He'd finished entering his notes and was rewatching the video of the mayor's announcement, since he'd missed a few parts the first time, when a flash of blue at the corner drew his gaze to Paige's coupe. Through the windshield, the sight of her cloud of red hair lifted his spirits, as did the bouncy strains of an oldie pop song resounding from her stereo.

After the car disappeared into the garage, Mike could have kicked himself for gawking. Not to mention missing part of the video all over again.

Paige cut across the patio carrying a large supermarket sack. "Roast chicken and vegetables," she called. "I brought plenty in case you're hungry."

"Sounds great."

She paused to study the moving figures on his laptop. "I can't stand that man!"

"Which one?"

"Hizzoner the mayor," she grumbled. "He was the swing vote on the halfway house. I'll never forget his smug look when he referred to us as 'that type of neighborhood.' As if the fact that we have small cottages and a lot of renters means we aren't entitled to security."

"I'm not one of his fans, either," Mike said. "Now about that chicken…"

They moved to the kitchen, falling into a comfortable rhythm as he set the table while she fixed iced tea. She was humming the song he'd heard playing in her car, and her green eyes sparkled.

"How'd your day go?" Mike asked.

"Lots of healthy babies and one of my fertility patients is pregnant." She set out the aromatic containers of food.

The news startled him. "Sheila?"

She blinked. "What, since yesterday?"

It did seem rather soon. Plus, he doubted she saw regular patients on a Sunday. "Must be someone on staff, which would explain why you ran into her on a weekend."

"Good guess." She didn't add any details, but that would be an invasion of the patient's privacy.

Mike had the same type of issue to deal with. He kept trying to figure out how to salvage his future chances for an endorsement even though his research was about to publicly humiliate Chief Walters. Paige's feedback about Mrs. Hightower had been right on target after he spoke about the case hypothetically. Why not do the same now?

Once they were seated and had taken the edge off their appetites, he spoke up. "I'd like your opinion about something."

She set down her fork. "Is this personal?"

"No, it's business. Why?"

"Between Dermot and my sisters, I've had enough personal drama for one day. I'm not sure I have the emotional energy to handle any more. But business would be okay." She took a second helping of steamed broccoli and cauliflower.

"You talked to your sisters." While Mike disliked the reminder that she might be moving out of state, he didn't want to be left in the dark. "What happened?"

"Long story. Let's get back to what's eating you."

Being shut out of her private life bothered him. But

he'd asked for that, hadn't he? Plus, now that he'd brought up his problem, might as well see it through.

Choosing his words carefully, Mike explained that he had to expose wrongdoing and, in the process, unintentionally harm a third party whose high opinion he valued. "He might be important to my future business plans, plus I hate to embarrass him, but I don't see how to avoid it. My first obligation is to my client."

"Communication might soften the blow. Would your client agree to give this guy a heads-up, or would that spoil your plans?" She regarded him sympathetically.

Mike hated being blindsided, and no doubt the chief did, too. Now that he thought about it, they should notify the local police first anyway. "You're a genius," he said. "Don't go to Texas. I rely on your advice."

"You can email me," Paige joked. "I promise not to bill you."

He felt a jolt of alarm. "Have you definitely decided to leave?"

"Still pending."

Relief. But short-lived unless he made her see how much she would regret moving, and not only because—he hoped—she'd miss him as much as he'd miss her. "Judging by what you've told me, your family will drive you crazy. I'm sure they're fine in small doses, but pretty soon you'll feel trapped and hemmed in. Like you don't know who you are anymore."

She peered at him through lowered lashes. "That sounds like the way you feel about becoming a father. Am I right?"

She understood him all too well. "That doesn't make me wrong about you and your family," he countered.

Paige sat there looking beautiful and sorrowful, like a

painted madonna come to life. "I'll decide by the end of the month. How's that?"

"You're asking my permission?"

"No. But I did promise you could stay for the summer. And since it's your baby, even though you're not responsible, I'll give you a fair chance to weigh all considerations."

He reached across the table to take her hand. "Paige, leaving here would be a mistake. For your own happiness."

She waited. Hoping he'd give her a personal reason to stay? The words refused to come.

If it were only a matter of the two of them... But she'd been right about what fatherhood meant to him. A twenty-year prison sentence. "I'll get the ice cream from the freezer." Mike arose and, as the moment passed, imagined he heard a door shutting, leaving him outside.

Outside of prison, he reminded himself, and rummaged through a drawer for the scoop.

Chapter Sixteen

"You're the most terrific doctor in the world!" Sheila Obermeier beamed at Nora from the examining table. "This has to be record time."

"It certainly happened fast." Reaching out, Paige helped her patient sit up. "Congratulations. And please credit Dr. Rattigan, too."

Less than three weeks after Gil received an injection for his low hormone count, the couple had achieved a pregnancy. It wasn't even the end of July, by a few days. Paige was more aware than usual of time passing because of her self-imposed deadline to reach a decision.

The petite woman tugged the hospital gown tighter. "If not for your advice, Gil would never have agreed to see Dr. Rattigan."

"Is everything okay between you two?"

"Yes. Actually, things are better than they've been in a long time. He was embarrassed when it turned out his hormones were low, but I remembered what you said about stroking his ego. So I told him that my hormones fluctuate all the time."

"Good response." Paige admired the woman's quick thinking.

"He's decided to join a gym and get in shape," Sheila noted. "I think you were right about him feeling inadequate compared to Mike. You know, they have more in common than I realized. They're both old-fashioned masculine guys, even though they show it in different ways. How're things going with him, by the way? I got the impression you two were involved."

Paige didn't like to discuss her personal life with a patient. Dodging the issue struck her as futile, though. "Nothing long-term. As you know, he doesn't want kids, and I do." Carefully, she added, "In fact, I'm expecting a baby. By choice." Word of Paige's condition had spread through the hospital these past few weeks, it being almost impossible to hide the signs of pregnancy from the nurses.

"It isn't his?"

"I used the sperm bank." That was true, as far as it went.

"How did he react to that?" Sheila asked.

"As I said, our long-term goals don't mesh." Enough about Mike. "Now, let's discuss your prenatal care."

By the time Sheila departed laden with pamphlets and vitamin samples, it was a few minutes past five o'clock. Paige went to check with her nurse. Although Sheila was the last scheduled patient, there was usually someone who had to be worked in on a Thursday with the weekend fast approaching.

However, Keely informed her that the waiting room was empty. "Now that there are two doctors, you're caught up." The heavyset nurse fiddled with a chart. "That temp nurse is doing okay for Dr. Franco, I suppose."

"I hear she's fine." When Nora returned to work a few weeks earlier, she'd brought in a temporary staffer until Bailey returned or gave notice. Still, Paige had to be fair about this. "I'd understand if you'd rather work with Dr. Franco than with me. We arranged things this way because you and I are both full-time."

The woman's dour features seemed to be fighting a battle. Finally the tiniest hint of a smile broke through. "I'd rather stay with you. I hope you aren't planning to leave. I heard you might be."

Lately, Paige had been missing family less and seeing more reasons to stay. Yesterday, she'd been surprised by the heartfelt swell of applause at a staff meeting when Dr. Tartikoff announced that Paige had moved into second position in the contest, ahead of Mark Rayburn and Zack Sargent. Then there'd been Cole Rattigan's admiring remark when, after thanking her for referring Gil Obermeier, the renowned urologist had said he was impressed with how much she cared about her patients.

Staying in California would be lonely at times. No sisters around to pinch-hit with the baby and, unless Mike chose to tell his folks, no connection to them, either.

Yet the grumpy nurse's unexpected vote of confidence seemed to fit a puzzle piece into place. With a profound sense of relief, Paige announced, "Actually, Keely, I've decided to stay here. My family's great but they can be overwhelming. I'll be happier going it alone."

"You won't be alone," the nurse said. "The people around here are like a family."

Paige barely hid her astonishment. Grim-faced Keely had antagonized Dr. T during a brief stint in his office and, whenever she joined a table of other nurses in the cafeteria, sat scowling as if she disapproved of their chitchat. Who would have guessed how she felt about them?

"Yes, they are," Paige agreed.

"And you're a big part of that."

From Keely, that amounted to high praise. "I'm glad you like working for me," Paige said.

"You're not fluttery like some of the other women doctors, and you're not bossy like the men." Keely had circulated as a temp for much of the time she'd worked at Safe Harbor, Paige had heard. "I like it here."

"Great." She gave the nurse a hug. After a moment's hesitation, Keely hugged her back.

Afterward, in her office, Paige was collecting her purse when Nora popped in, her face alight. "Sorry for eavesdropping but I overheard you and Keely. I'm glad you're staying!"

"Sign me up," Paige responded cheerfully.

"I don't mean to be nosy…."

"You mean about Mike?"

"Well, yes."

"I wish I could say there were romantic considerations, but that isn't it." Paige waved her friend into a chair. "I grew up afraid of getting lost in other people's ideas of who I was. But when the reality sank in that I'm going to be a single mother facing the future alone, I got scared. Turned out to be temporary. It's not like me to run from a challenge."

"You aren't staying because you feel you have to prove anything, are you?" Nora probed. "Because you're one of the most popular and respected doctors at the hospital."

"Thank you. That means a lot." Paige laughed, amazed at how free she felt. "I do feel like I belong here. And who knows? Maybe someday I'll meet the right guy."

Nora didn't say anything about Mike. And much as she liked her new partner, Paige wasn't about to volunteer anything further about the private, tender and very painful place in her soul that belonged to him.

"How about sharing a bottle of sparkling apple juice to celebrate our new partnership?" Nora asked. "I have some at home."

"You're on." Out they went, together.

ALTHOUGH HE'D WORKED for Kendall Technologies for almost a year and a half since buying Fact Hunter Investigations, Mike had never been invited to the owner's home until Thursday evening. As he parked near the harbor, he wished he knew what this meant.

Three weeks ago, Reese had received the report on the Doug Loughlin interview with fury. Outraged by the mayor's thievery, he'd been eager to go straight to the FBI, but had listened to Mike's urging that they take the case first to Jon Walters. Finally, he'd agreed.

"I realize you'd prefer to avoid antagonizing your former boss," Reese had said. "I've met the man a few times myself, and I respect him. But he's close to Roy. If he tips off the mayor and screws this up, I'll hold you responsible when the FBI goes Dumpster-diving through my files."

Mike had almost regretted putting himself on the line. On the other hand, he wasn't just doing this for himself. In a theft case—even one with international implications— he considered it proper to notify the local police first. So with Reese's permission, he'd called the chief and, after he explained that this was a sensitive matter, Walters had met them at Kendall Technologies.

In Reese's plush office, Mike had broken the news to the chief. He'd explained about the theft of a prototype medical tool by a Russian company, and laid out Doug's testimony. He'd also mentioned Roy's close association with Yelena.

"How close?" the chief had demanded.

"Closer than it should be. Beyond that, I'm bound by confidentiality to another client," Mike had said, and noted a scowl darkening Reese's face. They'd never discussed this particular matter before because it hadn't come up.

"We're talking about a crime," the chief had pointed out.

"And I'll testify if necessary. But the FBI can do a more thorough job of investigating than I can," Mike had said. "Anything I know, they'll find out for themselves."

"I hope they'll keep in mind that my company is the injured party here," Reese had added.

His manner guarded, the chief had thanked them both and promised to call in the FBI. A few days later, both Jon and Reese had sat in as Mike presented his findings to a pair of stony-faced agents. If the FBI had talked to any of the parties since then, no one had notified Mike.

Then today, Reese's secretary had issued a summons to meet him at home. While Mike supposed he ought to be flattered at the invitation, his instincts warned that his boss might simply want to ream him up and down without risk of corporate eavesdropping.

The scent of seaweed and the mewing of gulls accompanied Mike to the locked gate, where he pressed a button and announced his name. Through a pink tumble of bougainvillea, he made out the red-tile roof of the Mediterranean mansion Reese had purchased about a year ago for his bride.

The gate buzzed open. Mike strode onto a swirling expanse of brickwork punctuated by beds of flowers. Beyond the two-story house, he glimpsed a few sails traversing the harbor in the fading light. With a private dock, this place must have cost millions.

The maid who admitted him led the way through an arched doorway into an open area that was part entertainment center, part family room and part Middle Eastern bazaar stuffed with lamps and vases out of the *Arabian Nights*. Heavy brocade curtains obscured the glass doors overlooking the harbor, while velvet couches and clusters of small tables presented a maze en route to shaking hands with Reese and, unexpectedly, Jon Walters. Mike couldn't read either man's expression.

"You've met my wife, Persia." Reese presented the dark-eyed woman, clad in an embroidered silk top and flowing pants that failed to disguise her plumpness. In her early twenties, she hadn't snapped back from her recent pregnancy, but then, Mike didn't know much about new mothers. Come to think of it, Paige would look delicious with a few extra curves.

Mrs. Kendall offered him a limp hand. After a polite greeting, she said, "I'll go see how dinner is coming along."

The secretary hadn't mentioned dinner. Mike wasn't sure Reese expected him to stay, so, without comment, he gave her a faint smile and watched her go.

How strange that Reese had dumped his beautiful, accomplished first wife, Nora—now happily remarried and close friends with Paige—for a younger model with questionable decorating taste and a wimpy handshake. If the man had regrets, though, they didn't show.

Reese checked his watch. Mike could have told him the hour, since he'd arrived promptly at a quarter to seven, as requested. It seemed an odd time, which contributed to his sense of unease. Mike only liked surprises when he was the one springing them.

"I'll let the chief update you," the CEO said.

Mike turned to his former boss. If the boom was about to drop, he'd like to get it over with.

"The FBI's been keeping a lid on things, as you might expect," Jon told him with a hint of a twinkle in his pale eyes, or perhaps that was the effect of a garish ruby-tinted lamp dominating a nearby table. "However, I have my sources. I've learned that they've been investigating Yelena Yerchenko for quite awhile. Your tip gave them a break. It didn't take much to persuade Roy Hightower to cooperate, considering the kind of charges he could be facing."

Reese took another look at the watch. "We thought you might enjoy seeing this with us."

Mike refrained from asking what "this" referred to. He'd find out soon enough.

Reese fiddled with a remote, and a giant wall TV sprang to life. A few clicks connected them to the internet. On-screen, the name *On the Prowl in OC* yielded to a view of Ian Martin sitting across from Roy in the mayor's cramped city hall office. His doughy face shining with perspiration, Hightower clutched the edge of his desk as if preparing to duck behind it.

After introducing himself, the host said, "Safe Harbor Mayor Roy Hightower has an announcement to make. Your Honor, you have our full attention."

If Mike had ever seen a deer-in-the-headlights expression, this was it. "Well, Ian, I'm withdrawing from the assembly race. I realize it's only been a few weeks since I announced my candidacy, but—" his Adam's apple bobbed "—but there you have it."

"I'm sure our viewers would appreciate an explanation."

The mayor squirmed. "I've, uh, encountered some unforeseen financial problems. It will take all my attention to save my real-estate company and preserve the jobs of my employees. As you can see, I put loyalty to my workers ahead of my political plans."

"What a crock," Mike said before recalling where he was.

"I couldn't put it better myself." The chief leaned back on a couch, arms folded, watching the TV with dry amusement.

"How could you have been unaware of these problems as recently as a few weeks ago?" Ian pressed.

"I lost focus. Got caught up in my dedication to bettering the lives of my fellow citizens," Hightower babbled. "Serving as mayor is a major time suck...I mean commitment. As you know, it's a part-time position that only pays a modest sum. I took the job out of a dedication to public service."

"It comes with medical benefits, though. Aren't they worth more than the salary?" The host had obviously done his homework.

"Let's not get distracted." Beads of sweat stood out on the mayor's forehead. "Running for the assembly is a full-time job. My first responsibility is to my wife, who's always stood by me."

"I thought your first responsibility was to your employees," Ian said.

"Them, too." Hightower peered at someone off-camera. Gemma? "Well, I just want to thank the people who've supported me, like Chief Jon Walters, and apologize for letting them down."

After he stopped speaking, Ian let the silence lengthen. That was usually a good tactic for drawing people out, but the mayor simply sat there perspiring. Finally, the host faced the camera. "This is Ian Martin. Thanks for watching *On the Prowl in OC*."

As the image faded, Jon clapped ironically. "Guess that lets me off the hook."

"Eventually the whole story's bound to break," Mike pointed out.

Reese clicked off the screen. "I just hope the mayor doesn't get off easy." He didn't seem nearly as satisfied with this turn of events as the chief. But then, no matter what punishment the mayor might undergo, he'd never be able to pay restitution for what he'd cost Kendall Technologies. "On the plus side, we've offered to provide the FBI with all relevant documents, and they haven't asked for a general search."

"Glad to hear it," Mike said.

The maid reappeared. "Dinner is served in the dining room."

"Excellent. I hope everyone likes lamb. I left the menu up to my wife," Reese said as they arose.

Mike didn't, particularly, but he'd eat live snails rather than risk offending his best client. "Sounds tasty."

Jon quirked an eyebrow at him. Not a fan of lamb, either, evidently. "In case I haven't mentioned it, I appreciate your tactful hand in all this, Mike."

"Of course, my first responsibility is to preserve the jobs of my employees," he deadpanned. For a minute, he feared his irony was too obscure, and then both men chuckled.

He hadn't been entirely kidding, though. Successfully navigating this minefield meant a lot to the future of Fact Hunter Investigations.

Yet, as he took his place in the ornate dining room where the strains of Middle Eastern music played softly, Mike didn't feel the burst of contentment he'd expected. He'd dodged one bullet, and hurray for that. But Paige's decision about leaving had been looming over him all month, and the less she said about it, the more evident it became that she planned to go. He couldn't shake the sense that she was punishing him for not wanting to be a father.

Hell, he liked kids. These past weeks, he'd become more aware of them than ever—no surprise, considering he was practically surrounded.

Patty had stopped by work with her cute six-year-old

stepdaughter, who'd earnestly introduced Mike to a bandaged toy panda that he gathered had been the subject of the little girl's medical experiments. Then Lourdes had brought her two tots to the beach again, using the cottage as a staging area. While she and her toddler son were in the bathroom, Mike had read a picture book to Graciela, who'd curled trustingly on his lap. What a doll.

Yeah, kids were fine. No reason he couldn't stay friends with Paige and give her a helping hand now and then. Fair enough, considering it was biologically his kid. All the more reason for the child to grow up nearby.

Tonight, he'd thank her for the suggestion that had helped him keep both his client and an important business contact happy. Then he'd present his case in a logical, persuasive manner. Maybe she'd accept an offer for Mike to serve as, say, an honorary uncle.

It sounded like a reasonable plan. He only hoped it was enough incentive to keep her in Safe Harbor, where she belonged.

Chapter Seventeen

By the time the leisurely meal finished and Mike made his departure, it was nearly ten o'clock. He'd never enjoyed socializing with business acquaintances, but he masked his impatience in view of how important he considered these two men. Also, when Chief Walters relaxed and told a few jokes, he wasn't bad company. As for Reese, he proved jovial enough, but in Mike's opinion the good fellowship didn't run very deep.

As he was driving home it registered that, since Yelena was already on the FBI's radar, Mike would probably never have to disclose what he knew about her affair with Roy. No doubt their agents had pictures that put his snapshots to shame. He wouldn't have to break his promise to Mrs. Hightower.

The ring of his cell phone, wedged into its mount, yanked him out of his reflections. Pressing a key, he said into the headset he usually wore while driving, "Mike Aaron."

"Hi, there! It's me."

He instantly placed the irritating voice from his past. "Sheila. You're calling me why?" To hell with being polite. His ex-wife had crashed his family's picnic and now she was bugging him when he had better things to occupy his mind.

"Just wanted to share my wonderful news—I'm pregnant!"

"Good for you." *Now go away,* he thought as he turned onto Safe Harbor Boulevard.

"I thought you'd be happy for me." He heard a note of disappointment.

For Pete's sake, the woman had cheated on him. What did she expect? "It's great that you got what you wanted. But I'm still wondering why you're calling."

"Because I like Paige, and I thought I'd do you both a favor."

"A favor?" The only favor Mike wanted from his ex-wife was peace and quiet. Especially quiet.

"I don't want you to make the same mistake again," she went on. "Paige is a terrific person. I'd hate to see you break up over the same issue."

He knew he'd regret giving her the satisfaction, but he had to ask: "Whatever gave you that idea?"

"Something she said in her office today." He could picture the little blonde fiddling with her hair, the way she used to whenever she was nervous. "She told me all about how she got pregnant from the sperm bank."

"She did?" He'd never expected Paige to be so indiscreet.

"You ought to stick with her, Mike. She and I are both pregnant at the same time. That's fate, sending you a message."

What had Paige been thinking to share their secrets with Sheila—or anyone? "I don't believe in fate."

"Well you should." Sheila gave a little squeak. "Oh, Gil's back from the store. I gotta go."

"'Bye." When the light turned green, he hit the gas so hard the car lurched. Damn. Mike knew better than to let emotions affect his driving.

As he eased off on the gas, he remembered his plan to sweet-talk Paige. But how was he going to do that when she'd betrayed his trust?

Like it or not, his ex-wife had just thrown a monkey wrench into his plans.

AFTER TOASTING HER PLANS with Nora, Paige had been keyed up to share her decision with Mike. At home, when he didn't arrive by dinnertime, she'd considered calling, but that seemed too much like nagging.

They weren't married. While they *were* living together, that situation might be ending soon. In truth, she had no idea how to describe this relationship.

If only he wanted more. Sitting on the patio after eating a light meal, Paige watched an older couple stroll arm in arm along the sidewalk. A man to share her life with, a man to grow old with. That's what she longed for. With a pang, she recognized that she no longer wanted to meet Mr. Right, because she'd already found him. She'd never considered the possibility that when that happened, she might not be Ms. Right for him.

Did you ever hurt like this for anyone, Aunt Bree? She wished she could ask her aunt. There'd been a boyfriend who'd died in the Korean War, Paige recalled, but Bree hadn't said much about him.

Yet a conversation came back from the months when her aunt was growing frail. They'd been out here on the patio, Bree lying wearily in the lounger, her pale skin stretched tight across her cheekbones. "You can't always control the outcome of your choices." Sadness had shadowed her aunt's face. "You can only choose to the best of your ability. Then there'll be nothing to regret."

"Do you have any regrets?" Paige had asked.

She'd expected her aunt to say no. Instead, after a

moment, Bree had responded, "I closed my heart once because I never wanted to feel such pain again. I didn't mean that to be permanent, but I got used to keeping my feelings walled away. The years passed and now it's too late to change."

Tears had glistened on her aunt's cheek. Then a friend had stopped by for a visit, and they'd never returned to the subject. Paige wondered if Bree had been referring to her boyfriend's death.

I'm not like that. I won't close myself off.

If she had to go on without Mike, she'd pour her love into this baby. And hope that time healed hearts the way people claimed it did.

But she doubted it.

ON THE PATIO, MIKE WAS surprised to see Paige resting in a lounge chair in the dark. Then he took a step closer and realized she'd dozed off.

"Hey." Although she needed her sleep, he couldn't leave her out here. "You okay?"

Eyes flickering open, she stretched languidly. If he hadn't been so angry, he'd have drawn her into the house and the bedroom, caressing and kissing her until passion drove away her sleepiness.

And risk having her describe the whole scene to Sheila in the morning? Immediately, he dismissed the thought as unworthy. Still, she'd seriously damaged his trust.

"Where've you been?" Paige asked lazily.

"Excuse me?" He didn't like being called to account like a schoolboy.

"I waited for you." She swung her legs around and rose unsteadily.

"I never promised to be home any particular time." Spoiling for a fight, that's how he felt. His better judgment warned him to rein that in, but what had she been thinking to tell Sheila their secrets?

Paige wandered into the house. When she switched on a lamp, the light hurt his eyes.

"I didn't mean to sound bossy," she said. "I just had something to tell you."

"Does it have anything to do with you shooting off your mouth to my ex-wife?" Mike set his laptop case on the floor.

"What?" Brushing back a long strand of hair, she regarded him in confusion.

"She called a few minutes ago to tell me about her pregnancy and give me advice, if you can believe that. She claims that you and me having a child must be fate."

"So this concerns Sheila." Deep breath. "I need a cup of tea. How about you?"

"That doesn't even come close."

"Beer?" She ambled into the kitchen. Frustrated, he followed. Wasn't she going to apologize?

"I'm fine. Had a few drinks with friends." He left it at that.

Paige set about making tea. "Mike, I ask my patients a lot of personal questions, and it's hard to know where to draw the line when they ask questions in return, especially since Sheila saw us together at the picnic. Besides, my pregnancy isn't a secret."

"Is my paternity common gossip, as well?"

Frown lines striped her forehead. "Did she say that?"

"More or less."

"I told her I'd used donor sperm, but that's all."

Even so, she'd come too damn close to exposing a fact so deep and personal it cut to the bone. Anger rattled around seeking a target. "Are you going to be treating her through her entire pregnancy? Can I look forward to more of my personal life being revealed to my cheating ex-wife in little dribs and drabs?"

Paige poured the hot water over her teabag. "Sheila was Nora's patient originally. I could transfer her."

"I wasn't even planning to tell my own family." He rapped his knuckles on the door frame.

Steam from the tea misted Paige's eyes. "You really don't want anything to do with our baby, do you?"

"Our baby?" Even though he'd intended to stay involved, her question tightened the noose. "I didn't sign up for this. You made a decision all by yourself."

"I did." She tried to blow on the tea, but couldn't seem to manage. "Mike, about Sheila…"

"Let's not discuss her. You explained what happened. Fine." He supposed Paige wasn't exactly at fault, but his ex-wife's phone call had brought back feelings of anger and betrayal. "I'm in a bad mood and I'd rather not take it out on you, so let's just say good-night."

"I'm off to bed in a minute, anyway." Regarding him over the edge of the mug, Paige seemed pensive.

For a moment, as he turned away, he thought she was about to say something, but she merely gave him a half smile.

Tomorrow, after he calmed down, they should talk. But Mike had to admit, the likelihood of persuading her to stay in Safe Harbor seemed to dwindle by the minute.

PAIGE HAD SEEN SIMILAR miraculous sights hundreds of times, but never from this angle. Physically *or* emotionally.

"Can't tell the sex yet at eleven weeks, but he or she is an active little person." Mark Rayburn's dark eyes glowed with appreciation as he moved the ultrasound paddle across Paige's gel-covered stomach. On the monitor, a tiny baby whose head took up nearly half its length wiggled in a cone of light. "As you know, there is a blood test that can determine sex as early as seven weeks with ninety-five percent accuracy."

Paige had already decided against that. "There's still a five percent chance it's wrong. I'd rather wait until I can be more certain."

"I can't wait for my first ultrasound!" put in Lori. The nurse peered eagerly over Paige, who felt strange lying on the examining table, as if she should hop up and administer to the patient. "It's adorable. Do you have names picked out?"

"Bree for a girl and Brian for a boy." She wondered whether Mike would like those. *Uh-oh.* She'd been trying not to think about him, and now a rush of yearning flooded her. She ached for his dear, stern face to brighten with joy as he regarded this first, precious image of their child.

She had to get over this. Every time the subject of the baby came up, Mike withdrew even further. It was hopeless.

You can't make a man love you, and you certainly can't make him want to be a father.

All the same, she and Nora had discussed the problem with Sheila earlier. Her partner had gladly agreed to call and explain that she would be taking over the woman's maternity care. Nora planned to present it as a simple matter of resuming treatment of a longtime patient. Only if Sheila objected would she add that Paige felt an ethical conflict because of Mike.

Last night had been awkward and disappointing. Just when Paige hoped her decision to stay might spark a new closeness between them, Sheila's interference had created a rift. Obviously, Mike hadn't resolved his anger over the divorce.

This morning, Paige had rushed to the hospital early to deliver a patient's twins by Cesarean section. What a pleasure to see their little scrunched faces and hear the neonatologist announce that they were in excellent shape.

On the screen, she watched Baby B cavort without a care in the world. Six months from now, this little person would make his or her own debut.

Without a daddy.

A lump clogged Paige's throat. Too late, she recalled how clearly her emotions showed on her face. Mark and Lori moved about diplomatically keeping their remarks to practical matters. Although tempted to assure them everything was fine, Paige supposed that would only underscore the fact that things *weren't*.

But as Keely had pointed out, her coworkers and friends had become a family. She and Baby B would do just fine.

After thanking the doctor and nurse, Paige took the ultrasound photos in their protective envelope, and tucked them into a side pocket of her purse. In the car, she swung by the Suncrest Market to pick up groceries and returned home as the sunshine shaded into twilight.

On Seaside Lane, traffic was barely moving. Most likely that indicated an accident blocking the road up ahead, although Paige couldn't tell through the long line of cars. To avoid the mess, she turned right a few blocks before Seaside Court and wended her way via side streets.

Around the corner from her house, a motor home took up two spaces at the curb. As she passed the oversize vehicle, Paige glimpsed a man on the sidewalk. Pinched face, sly expression. Willy Kerrigan.

Another face appeared through the RV's windshield.

It was a newer resident, the man she'd seen casing parked cars with Willy. No way did he own that expensive RV.

As Paige reached for her cell phone, she saw the second man leap onto the sidewalk and start in her direction. A surge of alarm ran through her. *They know where I live.*

She couldn't dial and steer at the same time. Afraid to stop, Paige sped around the corner to her driveway before dialing 9-1-1, and then realized she should have kept going. Before she could back out, the men raced up, one blocking her escape while Willy headed for the driver's door.

She was trapped. No sign of Mike's car anywhere. Frantically, Paige spilled the facts to the dispatcher and hoped the police could get there fast.

"THIS IS WAY OVERKILL." Wiping sweat from his forehead, Mike surveyed the play structure he and Lock had spent the past few hours installing in his brother's rear yard.

A two-story fort, ladders and a tube slide to the ground, all for a baby that hadn't been born yet. The kit had promised easy assembly by two people. It hadn't mentioned heavy-duty drilling, hammering and hoisting that had left Mike with blistered hands and sweat soaking his coveralls. Still, this assemblage had to be incredibly fun. "I'd better test it to see if it's strong enough."

Lock finished driving bolts through predrilled holes in the slide and pushed a hank of wavy brown hair off his temple. "A big oaf like you? Forget it. I'll invite some of the neighborhood kids over."

Dropping onto a deck chair, Mike took a draft of the iced tea Erica had set out earlier. He and Lock had closed the office early, scoring a little hard-earned time off to install the play structure. He wished they'd had something like this while he was growing up.

Would Paige's baby ever play here? It seemed only fair that Mike's child…*her* child should enjoy what he'd helped assemble. Besides, why shouldn't she be invited over? Erica and Paige did work together.

As he imagined a little tyke scampering up that ladder and sliding gleefully down into Paige's outstretched arms, a knot formed in Mike's chest. It amazed him how much he wanted to share that moment. But fatherhood wasn't simply a matter of enjoying playtime or of suffering a few sleepless nights, either. It meant giving up control over his entire life.

"You really weren't going to tell me, were you?" Sweat beading his face, Lock stood back to admire their handiwork.

"Tell you what?"

"Come on, bro. It's all over the hospital that Paige is pregnant. Artificial insemination, that's the word." Lock quirked an eyebrow.

"That's right." Mike saw no need to elaborate.

"You guys make a great couple. I've never seen you so happy with anyone. I never cared much for Sheila." Following that blunt disclosure, Lock grabbed his own glass of iced tea and downed it in a couple of swallows.

"We going to discuss my love life? Because if we are, I'll leave and let you and Erica yammer about it."

"Okay, I don't claim to understand what's going on." The shorter man squinted into the fading light, studying the play fort. "But I think it's a shame you aren't sticking around. Unless she's throwing you out, of course."

"And why is this your business?"

Lock ignored the question. "Since you told me you have to find another place to live, I put two and two together."

"And got six or seven? I always said you needed remedial math."

"You used to want kids."

Now, that was ridiculous. "Did not."

"I remember you talking about what you'd do when you had a kid. How you'd teach him to play ball instead of spending too much time at video games. How you'd get a kick out of reading aloud from your favorite old picture books."

"You're confusing me with Denzel."

"Yeah, you guys look so much alike." Their brother had a rich chocolate complexion and stood about five foot eight.

"Nevertheless." To Mike, Lock was obviously making this stuff up. Or recalling something Mike had tossed out when the possibility of becoming a father sounded merely theoretical. "How old was I? Like, twenty?"

Lock snorted. "You told me that on your wedding day."

"Like hell I did!"

"You'd been dancing with Sheila, making goo-goo eyes at each other."

"Making what?"

"Don't you ever watch old movies?" Lock shook his head. "Hopeless. After you sat down, two little kids got up to dance together. They must have been about five. Totally earnest and concentrating on every step. Sheila went somewhere—to the bathroom with her mother, I think. You started talking to me about having kids."

This was ridiculous. "I did no such thing. I distinctly recall making it clear to Sheila when we were engaged that I didn't want children."

"Yeah, she told me that, and laughed about it. She said you didn't mean it. The word she used was *clueless*." Lock raised a hand to forestall a protest. "Which is one of the things I dislike about her. It's not right, mocking someone you're supposed to care about. But here's a reality check—every now and then you used to make some statement about how cute kids were."

"Grizzly cubs are cute, too. That doesn't mean I want to take one home."

"You said how you'd treat them differently from the way Mom and Dad treated us. More time for fun and games, fewer chores," Lock went on, unruffled.

"You're hallucinating." Grumpily Mike stared at the playhouse. "You're so awash in your wife's maternal hormones that you view the entire world through a pink haze."

"Blue haze," Lock corrected. "It's a boy."

"Yeah, but your wife's a girl."

"Last time I looked."

This conversation was becoming more absurd by the minute. "On that note, I'm heading home."

After a quick goodbye to Erica, Mike departed. The funny thing was, he thought as he drove, he did kind of remember those two children at his wedding reception. The little girl had belonged to one of Sheila's cousins and the little boy had been one of the Aarons' last foster children. A short while later, the boy's great-aunt and uncle had adopted him.

They really had been adorable, dancing together just like the grown-ups. Mike had felt utterly mellow that day. Having kids hadn't seemed like such a bad idea. When had that changed?

Maybe when things started to unravel with Sheila. Their quarreling and her pressure to rush into parenthood had made him feel cornered. In retrospect, Mike could see that at some level he'd registered that having children would bind him to her even more strongly.

Was that why he felt trapped every time he thought about being a father? Sheila wasn't his wife anymore. He needed to let go of whatever feelings she still provoked in him.

Easier said than done, but he liked the idea.

Just then, Mike hit a long line of traffic on the beach road. Annoyed, he rolled forward, his impatience growing by the minute until he reached Paige's street.

The moment he turned the corner and glimpsed the flashing bar atop the police cruiser, he forgot everything else.

Chapter Eighteen

Among the knot of people in front of Paige's house, Mike made out her tall figure, arms wrapped around herself, auburn hair cascading over her face. Was she all right?

As he parked and hurried toward the scene, Mike sorted out the figures. Officer George Granger was talking to Paige. Willy Kerrigan sat in the back of the cruiser, while Officer Bill Sanchez kept watch over another handcuffed man whom Mike recognized as Ben Eggers, a paroled burglar and drug user he'd checked out previously.

On the far side of the driveway, a couple of young men in Hawaiian-print shirts watched with folded arms. They were renters who'd moved in last Sunday. Not too noisy, so Mike had paid them little attention all week.

He reached Paige in a couple of long strides. "Are you okay?"

"Just a little shook up." The paleness of her skin made her freckles stand out. Mike wanted to kiss every one of them.

"What happened?"

"I saw those men breaking into an RV around the corner." Paige's voice trembled. *I should have been here to protect her, not loafing around with Lock*. "They followed me home. Luckily the police got here in just a minute."

"We were at an accident scene two blocks away. Now,

I need to take her statement," George said with a mean-
ingful look at Mike.

Much as he wanted to sweep Paige away from this
mess, he had to let the officer do his work. "I'll get you
a sweater from inside." The sea wind felt cold, and she'd
had a shock.

"Thanks," Paige said gratefully. "I'm glad you're here."

"So am I." The best Mike could do now was take care
of her. "Do you want me to put your purse in the house?"
It kept sliding off her shoulder.

"Oh, yes, thanks." Paige handed him the oversize bag.

Inside, as Mike set it on the sofa, he noticed a folder
jutting from a side pocket. On the tab was written Baby
Brennan.

How could he resist?

Drawing out the dark photograph, Mike glanced at the
tiny shape in the center. Big head. Cute little nose. Sweet
mouth.

A person. Real and whole. A little boy or girl who
someday was going to climb that ladder and slide down
the tube, laughing and shrieking.

Right into waiting arms. But whose would they be?
Paige's? Some other guy's? Absolutely not!

Mike had seen sonograms before. His sister Lourdes
had shown him Graciela's when she was pregnant and
Lock had waved one of these images around the office a
few weeks ago. Primarily out of courtesy, Mike had taken
a mild interest.

This baby was different. He ached to hold it, to see its
little face light up. To cuddle its soft body and hum to it.
*You're mine, you know that? I'm going to keep you safe
from creeps like Willy and Ben.*

But how could he do that if Paige moved to Texas?

Through the window, Mike saw her shivering as she

talked to George. Ashamed of himself for lingering, he returned the picture to its folder and fetched a cardigan from the front closet.

Outside, a second patrol car had pulled up to assist. "Thanks." Paige draped the sweater around her shoulders.

"We're just about done here." George flipped his notebook shut.

Another officer came over to fill them in about the RV. Window busted, alarm disabled. The owner, whom they'd located in the adjacent house, had found an iPod and an envelope of cash missing.

Bill produced an evidence bag containing those items. "We have a match."

That ought to be enough to send the men to prison on parole violations and possibly a new conviction, Mike reflected. But there'd be more shady types to take their places at the halfway house.

All the more reason for Paige to move away.

He had to figure out how to keep her here. To protect her and the baby. But Mike couldn't simply expect her to fall into his arms after what he'd said last night.

You really don't want anything to do with our baby, do you? she'd asked.

And what arrogant reply had he given? *I didn't sign up for this. You made a decision all by yourself.*

Damn. How was he going to atone for that?

His brain churned as he waited for the officers to finish, and then he escorted Paige inside. Understandably jittery, she ate only a few bites of dinner and excused herself for a nap. "I'm exhausted."

By contrast, Mike felt amped up and restless. "Will you be okay if I go for a walk? I'll set the alarm, of course."

She nodded. "Sure. While I like having you around, I'm not that fragile."

After cleaning up the kitchen, he changed into casual clothes and sandals. Then, peeking into Paige's bedroom and seeing her dozing beneath the covers, Mike nearly aborted his walk to stay and stand guard. But if he didn't burn off some energy, he'd explode. And a treadmill in that cramped garage just wasn't enough.

The last streaks of light colored the sky as he went out. The street lay quiet, and on the beach a few isolated groups of people sat enjoying the sunset. A handful of surfers, resembling seals in their glistening wet suits, rode the waves.

The wind nipped at Mike as he paced in the direction of the harbor. He had to bring order out of the chaos in his head.

Why hadn't he admitted before, even to himself, how much he loved Paige? He couldn't envision a future without her. But until today, that would have meant accepting a baby he didn't want.

Lock was right. In a way, Sheila had been, too. While Mike had been reluctant to have kids before marrying her, in time he'd probably have yielded. Instead, his doubts had hardened in reaction to her manipulations. Children would have yoked him to Sheila for a lifetime, regardless of whether they stayed married.

How utterly different things were with Paige. She was ready to let him go. Even tonight, after the scare she'd been through, she refused to tie him down.

Maybe his insight had come too late. What he needed was another flash of inspiration, to keep her and the baby safe.

And to keep them with me.

WHEN PAIGE AWOKE, SHE knew instinctively that Mike hadn't returned yet. The quiet house vibrated with his absence. Also, the light remained red on the duplicate alarm panel in her bedroom.

How long would it take before this place no longer felt incomplete without him? *Or am I the one who feels incomplete?*

Ashamed of her weakness, Paige fixed a cup of tea in Bree's airy kitchen, where pots of herbs that her aunt had planted still flourished in the greenhouse window. Stretching her legs under the table, she gazed out at the street, peaceful once again in the twilight.

Was this a weakness, to love a man so much that the prospect of losing him tore her apart? She'd simply have to get over it. Mike would never yield to persuasion. If anything, he grew more distant at anything that he interpreted as pressure.

They belonged together. But his heart didn't have room for their baby.

A tear slid down Paige's cheek. Embarrassed, she wiped it off. She was strong enough to weather this storm. She just wished she didn't have to be.

Outside, she glimpsed his powerful shape pacing along the sidewalk. Unbidden, her spirits lifted as, at the front door, she heard Mike remove his shoes and shake out the sand. He came in quietly, then saw her sitting in the kitchen. "You're awake."

"Just needed a nap." He couldn't see the trace of tears, could he? "I'm fine now."

He paused in the doorway, uncharacteristically hesitant. Finally he said, "I have an idea about the halfway house."

That was good. "I'm open to anything you can suggest." Setting aside her empty cup, Paige accompanied him into the front room. "What is it?"

"Let's get comfortable." He indicated the couch.

"Sure." Relaxing against the cushions, she watched him with an attempt at nonchalance.

Instead of sitting, he removed the smart phone from his pocket. "I've been doing a little research."

How odd. "On the beach?"

"Just checking something out." He frowned at something on the screen. "The escrow officer who handled the sale of the halfway house to its current owners was a woman named Yelena Yerchenko. She owns the escrow company next to my office."

"Okay." Although she didn't see why that mattered, Paige figured he was working up to that.

"I'm not at liberty to disclose the details, but I believe Mayor Hightower had a conflict of interest when he served as the swing vote on the council. He should have recused himself," Mike went on.

That sounded promising. "You think we could force a revote?"

"Possibly." Mike gave her a wry smile. "But there's an approach that might produce results a lot quicker. The company that owns the house has invested a lot of money. They won't want to risk losing their permit. After the arrest today, I'll bet they'd be willing to make a few changes, especially when I drop a hint about the mayor's conflict of interest. Would you accept a rehab facility as long as the occupants aren't ex-cons?"

"Sure." Paige sympathized with people trying to kick their drug and alcohol addictions.

"I'll get to work on it." Mike tucked the phone in his pocket. "Paige, I don't want you to move to Texas. If you feel safe here, will you stay?"

"That's not the reason I considered going." No sense delaying; she'd meant to tell him her decision last night, anyway. "I thought I needed family around me, but I've decided to stay here."

He looked startled. "You have?"

If she said she hoped he'd be involved with the baby, it might push him away. Better not to. "I've put down roots in Safe Harbor. This is my home now."

Mike blew out a breath. "I'm glad. More than glad. Paige, can you forgive me?"

"Forgive you for what?"

"Being an idiot," he said.

She chuckled. "I got over that a long time ago."

"I mean, about the baby."

She could hardly resent him for refusing to accept a child she'd conceived on her own. "You don't owe me anything."

"Please let me finish." He rushed on. "Paige, I love you and the baby, both. I know I haven't acted like it. I'll prove it to you, however long it takes."

She could hardly believe it. Had he really said the words she longed to hear, or was she misinterpreting? "Love isn't something you have to earn, Mike. Trust, yes, but you've never done anything to break trust with me."

"So I can stay here with you?" He shook his head as if he hadn't meant it. "No, wait."

Disappointment arrowed through her. She *had* misunderstood. "What?"

When he reached into his pocket again, she thought he was going to pull out the phone, although she couldn't imagine why. Instead, he produced a small dark shape and held it in his open palm.

"What's that?" Paige leaned forward.

"Sorry. The light's bad." Mike switched on a lamp and came to sit beside her. Holding up the small object, he angled it against the glow until it shone a brilliant shade of purple.

"Sea glass." Paige took it with a sense of awe. He hadn't borrowed it from her collection; she'd never seen this particular shape before. Naturally buffed, it formed a slightly misshapen diamond. "Where did you get this?"

"Just now, on the beach. If it weren't for a ray of sunlight, I'd never have noticed it." Mike studied her intently. "You told me once that your aunt promised to send you purple glass as a sign of approval or a nudge in the right direction. Is it fair to suggest I have your aunt's blessing to ask you to be my wife?"

Paige couldn't speak. Those darn tears were welling up again. Finally, she said, "I love you, Mike."

"Will you marry me?"

The knot in her stomach dissolved. "Yes!"

Mike glanced at the gemlike glass. "I could have this made into an engagement ring, surrounded by diamonds."

She had to ask one question. "What about the baby?"

"I love the baby, too. Did I leave that out?"

"No, but…how did this happen?" Before he could respond, she added, "I'll get a DNA test."

"Not necessary. It's mine. I know it in my heart, and frankly, I don't care anyway." He stroked her hair lightly. "I saw the sonogram. Paige, I love him. Or her. Do you have a name picked out?"

"Baby B." She gave him a tentative smile. "That stands for Bree or Brian. Is that okay?"

"Everything you do is okay," he said.

"Sounds good to me." Slipping her arms around Mike, Paige cuddled close. Before she knew it, he was kissing her forehead, her cheeks, the tip of her nose and her mouth as if he couldn't stop.

It felt wonderful.

THEY SET THE WEDDING DATE for early September, planning a simple ceremony with immediate family and close friends. That still made for a long list.

In her happiness, Paige almost forgot that there might be one person for whom their joyful news would prove unpleasant. Then one day in late August, as she was on her way to lunch, she ran into Sheila Obermeier in the hall outside the office. The short blonde was leaving also.

Paige gave herself a mental kick. Nora had told her that Sheila had an appointment that morning, but Paige hadn't taken note of the time. Still, she couldn't avoid the woman forever.

"How're things going with Dr. Franco?" she asked as they walked toward the elevator.

"Good, I guess. I like both of you about the same." Sheila's forehead furrowed. "I hear you and Mike are getting married."

It wasn't like Nora to gossip. But then, Sheila might have heard the news any number of places, considering that she knew Mike's family. "Yes." At the elevator, Paige pressed the down button.

"Did you really get pregnant through artificial insemination?"

"I did," Paige confirmed.

"And he's marrying you anyway?"

She heard the pain in Sheila's voice. Despite everything that had happened, the woman harbored feelings for her ex, or perhaps this was a matter of insecurity. "Thank you for giving him some straight talk."

The doors opened. "Did that really help?" Sheila asked as they stepped into the empty elevator.

"I think you had an impact," Paige said.

Sheila brightened. "I'm glad."

The elevator glided downward. "Now we both get happy endings," Paige noted.

"Don't you mean happy beginnings?" Sheila asked as they reached the lobby.

"Exactly." Paige liked that phrasing.

"Listen." Sheila stopped in the middle of the lobby. "You should feel free to compare notes with me anytime. I've learned a lot about handling men."

"I can see that." Paige appreciated the good intentions. "Thanks."

"'Bye!" Sheila beamed as she walked away.

Paige had to admit she had no idea how to handle Mike. And she intended to keep it that way.

IN A GLOWING CIRCLE OF LIGHT from the bedside lamp, Paige tried to read a medical journal. Tonight, though, she just couldn't focus, not with Mike ensconced beside her in his crisp striped pajamas, laptop on his knees, working intently.

She plucked a bit of lint from his sandy hair. When he looked up, she said, "Sorry. I didn't mean to disturb you."

"That's okay." He closed the laptop. "I meant to tell you something at dinner but we were interrupted." His parents had stopped by unexpectedly on the way home from visiting friends. Between catching up on wedding plans and sharing family news, the evening had flown by.

"What's that?" Paige waited for him to continue.

"I decided to stop donating sperm." He cleared his throat. "It seemed like a good idea at the time but... well..."

"No explanation necessary." Besides, she had a small confession to make. "I know you said it didn't matter, but I ran a DNA test using the last sample of your sperm. The baby's definitely yours. I should have asked you first because if it had turned out not to be…"

His fingers brushed her cheek. "When I said it didn't matter, I meant it. Now, any other revelations? This seems to be the night for them."

She hadn't had a chance to mention Sheila's visit, Paige realized. "I ran into your ex-wife at lunchtime. She made me promise to ask for advice in dealing with you, if I need any."

He grinned. "Do you?"

"I'd say I've done just fine without it."

She held out her left hand, where the purple centerpiece on her ring shone as brightly as the diamonds around it. Everywhere she went, people commented on it. To their questions, Paige described the purple glass as a family heirloom, which was what she considered it.

"Okay, now that we've taken care of business, look at this." Reopening the laptop, Mike swung it toward her. The screen displayed beach-oriented baby decor. "What do you think?"

She loved the theme. "Look at that cute mermaid mobile!"

Mike frowned. "I was thinking more of the surf's-up theme."

"It's cheerful," Paige conceded. "But I could live without the surfboard wall decals."

"They're nice and bright." He sounded disappointed.

"The surf's-up sheets only come in blue."

"That's the color of the ocean. And lots of girls surf." He sighed. "I suppose we should table this discussion until we know the sex for sure."

Although Paige never knew how he'd react to teasing, she decided to go for it. "Or we could have more than one baby."

Mike froze. In the silence, she heard the low beat of rock music from their neighbors. At last, he squeezed out the words, "It's a small house."

"I'm joking," she said.

Instead of meeting her gaze, Mike returned his attention to the laptop. A few clicks later, he turned the screen so she could see.

Bunk beds.

"We could buy a set of these when the kids get bigger." He quirked an eyebrow. "If I survived sharing a room, so can they."

Incredible. Curling close to him, Paige murmured, "Just imagine making a baby the old-fashioned way."

"Oh?" he said. "Which way is that?"

She closed his laptop and set it on the nightstand beside them. "Let me show you."

"I always appreciate a demonstration. It helps me get the hang of things," Mike said, and turned off the light.

* * * * *

HEART & HOME

Harlequin®

American Romance®

COMING NEXT MONTH
AVAILABLE MAY 8, 2012

#1401 A CALLAHAN WEDDING
Callahan Cowboys
Tina Leonard

#1402 LASSOING THE DEPUTY
Forever, Texas
Marie Ferrarella

#1403 THE COWBOY SHERIFF
The Teagues of Texas
Trish Milburn

#1404 THE MAVERICK RETURNS
Fatherhood
Roz Denny Fox

REQUEST YOUR FREE BOOKS!

2 FREE NOVELS PLUS 2 FREE GIFTS!

Harlequin®

American ★ Romance®

LOVE, HOME & HAPPINESS

YES! Please send me 2 FREE Harlequin® American Romance® novels and my 2 FREE gifts (gifts are worth about $10). After receiving them, if I don't wish to receive any more books, I can return the shipping statement marked "cancel." If I don't cancel, I will receive 4 brand-new novels every month and be billed just $4.49 per book in the U.S. or $5.24 per book in Canada. That's a saving of at least 14% off the cover price! It's quite a bargain! Shipping and handling is just 50¢ per book in the U.S. and 75¢ per book in Canada.* I understand that accepting the 2 free books and gifts places me under no obligation to buy anything. I can always return a shipment and cancel at any time. Even if I never buy another book, the two free books and gifts are mine to keep forever.

154/354 HDN FEP2

Name   (PLEASE PRINT)

Address   Apt. #

City   State/Prov.   Zip/Postal Code

Signature (if under 18, a parent or guardian must sign)

Mail to the **Reader Service:**
IN U.S.A.: P.O. Box 1867, Buffalo, NY 14240-1867
IN CANADA: P.O. Box 609, Fort Erie, Ontario L2A 5X3

Not valid for current subscribers to Harlequin American Romance books.

Want to try two free books from another line?
Call 1-800-873-8635 or visit www.ReaderService.com.

* Terms and prices subject to change without notice. Prices do not include applicable taxes. Sales tax applicable in N.Y. Canadian residents will be charged applicable taxes. Offer not valid in Quebec. This offer is limited to one order per household. All orders subject to credit approval. Credit or debit balances in a customer's account(s) may be offset by any other outstanding balance owed by or to the customer. Please allow 4 to 6 weeks for delivery. Offer available while quantities last.

Your Privacy—The Reader Service is committed to protecting your privacy. Our Privacy Policy is available online at www.ReaderService.com or upon request from the Reader Service.

We make a portion of our mailing list available to reputable third parties that offer products we believe may interest you. If you prefer that we not exchange your name with third parties, or if you wish to clarify or modify your communication preferences, please visit us at www.ReaderService.com/consumerschoice or write to us at Reader Service Preference Service, P.O. Box 9062, Buffalo, NY 14269. Include your complete name and address.

HARI1B

The heartwarming conclusion of

from fan-favorite author

TINA LEONARD

With five brothers married, Jonas Callahan is under no pressure to tie the knot. But when Sabrina McKinley admits her bouncing baby boy is his, Jonas does everything he can to win over the woman he's loved for years. First the last Callahan bachelor must uncover an important family secret…before he can take the lovely Sabrina down the aisle!

A Callahan Wedding

**Available this May
wherever books are sold.**

www.Harlequin.com

HAR75405

After a bad decision—or two—Annie Mendes
is determined to succeed as a P.I. But her first assignment
could be her last, because one thing is clear: she's not cut
out to be a nanny. And Louisiana detective Nate Dufrene
seems to know there's more to her than meets the eye!

Read on for an exciting excerpt of the upcoming book
WATERS RUN DEEP by Liz Talley…

THE SOUND OF A CAR behind her had Annie scooting off the road and checking over her shoulder.

Nate Dufrene.

Her heart took on a galloping rhythm that had nothing to do with exercise.

He slowed beside her. "Wanna ride?"

"I'm almost there. Besides, I wouldn't want to get your seat sweaty."

His gaze traveled down her body before meeting her eyes. Awareness ignited in her blood. "I don't mind."

Her mind screamed, *get your butt back to the house and leave Nate alone.* Her libido, however, told her to take the candy he offered and climb into his car like a naughty little girl. Damn, it was hard to ignore candy like him.

"If you don't mind." She pulled open the door and climbed inside.

The slight scent of citrus cologne, which suited him, filled the car. She inhaled, sucking in cool air and Nate. Both were good.

"You run often?" he asked.

"Three or four times a week."

"Oh, yeah? Maybe we can go for a run together."

Her body tightened unwillingly as thoughts of other things they could do together flitted through her mind. She shrugged as though his presence wasn't affecting her. Which it *so* was. Lord, what was wrong with her? *He* wasn't her assignment.

"Sure." No way—not if she wanted to keep her job. As he parked, she reached for the door handle, but his hand on her arm stopped her. His touch was warm, even on her heated flesh.

"What did you say you were before becoming a nanny?"

Alarm choked out the weird sexual energy that had been humming in her for the past few minutes. Maybe meeting him on the road wasn't as coincidental as it first seemed. "A real-estate agent."

Will Nate discover Annie's secret?
Find out in WATERS RUN DEEP by Liz Talley,
available May 2012 from Harlequin® Superromance®.

And be sure to look for the other two books
in Liz's THE BOYS OF BAYOU BRIDGE series,
available in July and September 2012.